A MIDWIFE'S CHRISTMAS

Midwife Maudie and Detective Sergeant Dick Bryant are settling into parenthood, preparing for baby Charlie's first Christmas. But this December will prove to be one of the most eventful in memory. An unknown assailant is attacking multiple Father Christmases. A vulnerable young girl is missing, thrown out by her father in disgrace. And Dick's patience with Maudie's interference in police cases is wearing thin. Meanwhile, there are the politics of the village nativity play to contend with — from protecting soloists' fragile egos to wrangling live farmyard animals. Then a shocking event puts Charlie in danger . . .

CATRIONA McCUAIG

A MIDWIFE'S CHRISTMAS

A Midwife Maudie mystery

Complete and Unabridged

LINFORD
Leicester

First published in Great Britain in 2014

First Linford Edition
published 2016

A catalogue record for this book is available
from the British Library.

ISBN 978–1–4448–3025–5

Published by
F. A. Thorpe (Publishing)
Anstey, Leicestershire

Set by Words & Graphics Ltd.
Anstey, Leicestershire
Printed and bound in Great Britain by
T. J. International Ltd., Padstow, Cornwall

This book is printed on acid-free paper

1

Maudie Bryant was not having a good day. Baby Charlie had kept them awake all night, grizzling, and his faithful guardian, Rover, had added to the misery by giving vent to mournful howls that echoed through the house. As she walked the floor with her unhappy little son, Maudie thought ruefully about all the knowledgeable advice she'd given to other new mothers about the management of newborns. Now, she was desperate for sleep, and would cheerfully have handed her child over to some passing gypsy with instructions to take him far away and let her rest!

She had just settled him in his cot and returned to bed when he started up again.

'Can't you keep him quiet, love?' Dick moaned, rolling over in bed and taking most of the blankets with him. 'I've got to go to work in the morning, you know.'

'I'm doing my best,' his wife told him

between gritted teeth, fumbling for her slippers and only finding one. 'I can't think what's the matter with him. It can't be teething at his age.'

'Probably wind,' Dick muttered. 'Have you burped him?'

Maudie swallowed a rude retort and stumbled towards the nursery. Charlie's napkin was soaking. She changed him and put him down again. 'Let's hope that works!' she whispered as she tiptoed to the door. She had just stretched out beside her husband when the wails began again. With a groan, she pulled her pillow over her head.

Now it was morning and the sun was shining in at the kitchen window. Charlie was blissfully asleep at last, and Maudie made use of the blessed peace by making a mound of scrambled eggs for Dick's breakfast.

His eyes lit up when he wandered into the kitchen, bleary-eyed. 'Scrambled eggs! Good-oh! Is that all for me, love?'

'I'm having some, too. In case you've forgotten, it's the mother-and-baby clinic today, and you said I could get a lift into

Midvale with you when you go to work.'

Dick pulled a face. 'Is that today? Can't you give it a miss for once? I've a lot on today, and I ought to get going as soon as I've downed that lot.'

'No, I can't give it a miss. I want someone to have a look at Charlie, in case he's sickening for something.'

Grumbling, Dick slathered butter on the pile of toast Maudie handed him, and passed a slice back to her. 'Come and sit down, love. Get that inside you and you'll feel a bit brighter.'

The tears came to Maudie's eyes as she accepted the small love token from her husband. Other women might crave diamonds and mink coats as proof of their husbands' affection, but she was grateful for a kind word on a sunny morning. She wondered how many marriages were put at risk by a baby who just wouldn't stop crying. The shameful thought came to her that she could understand those parents who, driven mad by crying that would not stop, harmed their children in a flare of temper. She must pull herself together!

3

'I suppose I'd better go and get him up,' she told Dick, who was wiping his plate clean with a toast crust.

'And unless you mean to come to Midvale in your nightie, I suggest you go and put some clothes on,' he said. 'I'll be ready for the off in ten minutes.'

Maudie, yearning for a long soak in a lavender-scented bath, nodded agreement. The tender moment was over and real life had intruded.

Baby Charlie was blissfully asleep, looking rosy and angelic in his cot. 'Little monkey!' Maudie murmured, scooping him up. 'You've given your poor mum a beast of a night, and no mistake!' For two pins, she'd give the clinic a miss and get back to bed while the going was good, but duty called. As a midwife she had conducted such clinics herself, and so she was quite capable of keeping an eye on her own child's progress. Still, she valued attending one on Charlie's behalf because it was important for him to receive his immunization jabs at the appropriate time and to have his weight recorded.

4

Besides, it did her good to chat to other mothers. After being free as the air while she'd toured the district on her trusty bicycle, visiting patients and delivering babies, she was now largely confined to home with her own baby. She found that she missed the exchange of gossip that had accompanied her daily round.

She smiled down at her wriggling son as she buttoned him into his little matinee coat and reached for his pram suit.

'Are you coming, love? Time's getting on,' Dick called.

An ominous smell filled the air. Maudie sighed. 'What am I going to do with you, Charlie Bryant? No time to give you a bath, my lad. We'll have to make do with a lick and a promise.' She filled a basin with warm water and began again.

Dick appeared in the doorway. 'If you don't get a move on, I'll have to go without you,' he muttered.

'I'm coming, I'm coming!' Maudie growled, applying talcum powder to their son's bottom. 'I'll have to finish dressing this one in the car, that's all.'

At last they were on their way. Maudie

caught a glimpse of herself in the rear view mirror, and didn't like what she saw. A middle-aged woman with frizzy hair and no makeup. The beauty editor of her favourite women's magazine would have something to say about that! You were supposed to leap out of bed in the morning and do marvellous things to your face before your husband caught sight of you. Otherwise he would be driven straight into the arms of some glamorous secretary he met on the job.

She fumbled in her bag for a tube of lipstick. She was carefully applying a layer of Scarlet Passion when the car went over a bump and the lipstick smeared all over her upper lip. With a sigh, she spat delicately on her clean hankie and began to repair the damage.

* * *

The clinic was teeming with mothers, babies, and assorted toddlers when Maudie arrived, clutching her son. She sank down in the only remaining empty seat, fortunately located at the end of a row of chairs, smiling at her neighbour as she did so.

'Am I glad to see you,' the woman remarked. Maudie looked at her more closely.

'Er, have we met before?' How shameful if this was a former patient and she hadn't recognized her. She stared rather rudely at the dowdy woman, who was holding an overweight baby on her lap. Wisps of grey hair escaped from fat pink rollers protruding from a ragged scarf, done up turban-style. Unlike Maudie, she had made an effort with pancake makeup, and two red blotches on her cheeks bore witness to a heavy-handed application of rouge.

'No, no,' the vision said. 'I mean, look at all them mums! Not a day over twenty, some of them: just bits of girls. Nothing wrong with that, of course, but it makes me feel a bit silly, see, sitting here like a bump on a log. It's all right now you've come. Two grannies together, that's us!' She grinned, showing a gap between her two front teeth.

'Grannies?' Maudie stammered.

'Yes, this is our Sandra's Darren. I mind him while she's at work down the shoe factory. Her hubby didn't want her going back to work — reckoned it makes him look like a poor provider — but she would have it. Saving up for a place of their own, they are. Been living with us ever since they got married, see. Well, you know what it was like after the war; you couldn't find a place to rent for love nor money. They moved into our spare room. Not that I minded that, really. It was all right till this one came, and then it got a bit much with him crying day and night.'

'I can imagine.'

The woman turned her gaze on Charlie, who was busily trying to pull a button off Maudie's coat. 'So who's this, then? Your daughter's child, is it?'

'I don't have a daughter.'

'Ah, then it's your daughter-in-law's baby, is it? Do they live with you and your hubby, then?'

'Darren Wilmott!' Maudie was saved from the necessity of a reply by the appearance of a young nurse with a clipboard hugged to her chest.

'That's us,' the woman said, struggling to her feet. 'Nice meeting you, I'm sure!'

Charlie held up his little arms to the woman, babbling something that sounded suspiciously like *Mama*, although at four months old he was rather too young for that.

'Ah, the pretty dear!' the woman cooed, reaching out to pat him on the head. 'Make the most of him while they're staying with you, love. They grow up too fast, I always say.' She trundled off, with Darren Wimott peering over her shoulder.

'Thank you very much, Charlie Bryant!' Maudie said to herself. 'Behaving as if you agreed with the old trout! There's nothing like a bit of family loyalty! Another granny, indeed!'

Of course, it wasn't everyone who gave birth for the first time at the age of forty-two, as Maudie had. And if she had married in her teens or early twenties, as some of her old school friends had, she might well be a gran by now! She could hardly blame the woman for her false assumption. So why did it sting so much?

Perhaps it was time for a makeover.

Already Dick had asked what she'd like in terms of a Christmas present; she might ask him to fund a new hairdo and a facial. She thought about the pitifully few items of makeup on her dressing table at home; those should be replenished.

During her days as a district midwife she had seldom used cosmetics. A daily round of cycling for miles in the wind and rain hardly made the effort worthwhile. And since the advent of Charlie, when she always seemed to have her hands in water, she had more to worry about than chipped nail varnish. Whenever she had money to spare, her favourite glycerine and rosewater hand lotion seemed more important than mascara and vanishing cream. After all, you mustn't handle a baby with rough skin!

That invisible beauty editor at Ladies World was famous for pouring scorn on readers who had Let Themselves Go. She would certainly have something to say if she could see Maudie now!

2

In his office at Midvale, Dick Bryant looked up from the case notes he was reading to find a familiar figure standing on the other side of his desk.

'Is that you, Sarge? I didn't expect to see you here again, now you've retired. Have you come to report a crime?'

The older man mopped his brow. 'Just lock me up in a nice comfy cell, will you, Bryant? And fetch me a cup of tea to go with it.'

Dick laughed. 'Sit down, mate, and I'll see what we can do in the tea department. What's the matter with you, anyway? You look done in.' He beckoned to a passing policewoman, lifting a hand to his lips in the unmistakable gesture of raising a teacup. She nodded and passed on.

Ex-sergeant John Fry groaned. 'You see before you the sad remains of Father Christmas, worn to a shadow by attending to the demands of the younger generation. A more spoiled lot of kiddies you never did meet.'

'What on earth are you talking about?'

'I've been working in Father Christmas's Grotto, haven't I? In Bentham's department store. In the run-up to the day, they have a Father Christmas on duty to listen to what the kiddies want as presents, and that's me. They come and sit on my lap, and I'm supposed to nod and smile while a photographer snaps us. That's another money-spinner for the shop, of course. The fond mamas can order copies of the photos to send to Granny; pure profit for Bentham's.'

The policewoman returned with a mug of tea, which she handed to the unhappy Father Christmas. He slurped down some of the murky liquid as if he had just arrived at an oasis after a week in the desert.

'That doesn't sound too bad to me,' Dick said, trying to hide a smile. 'But why are you doing this, Sarge?'

Fry rolled his eyes. 'I need the money, don't I! My pension doesn't go far, and the wife is set on having the kitchen done up. Like you, I thought this would be money for old rope — but not a bit of it! It's worse than being in the war. I'd happily face Rommel in North Africa again rather than those little devils.'

Now Dick couldn't contain his laughter. 'It can't be that bad, surely?'

'No? Then think again, mate. One of them wet on my lap the other day, and I had to go home on the bus with my trousers wringing wet. I got some very funny looks, I can tell you! Then, do you see this black eye of mine? That was another of the little dears.

' "You're not the real Father Christmas,' he says. 'The real one is in Gloucester, I know 'cause I saw him when we went there last week to visit my Nan. You're just pretending to be him, and I'm going to tell everybody you're a nasty man who ought to be put in prison.' "

'Oh, dear!'

'Well, we're supposed to treat the little dears with kid gloves, so I played along. I said that Father Christmas has to work all over the place; so I was in Gloucester last week right enough, and now I'm in

13

Midvale, and what would he like for Christmas? 'No you're not him!' he yells, and socks me right in the eye. Believe me, it was all I could do not to turn him over my knee and give him six of the best, but I managed to restrain myself. I did say a few choice words to his mother, though, and she dragged him away without a word of apology. Then I had this little miss who whispered in my ear a list of presents as long as my arm, ending with a Shetland pony!

''I don't think Father Christmas can bring you all that,' I told her. 'He has to save something for all the other little girls and boys.' She looked me straight in the eye — the good one, not the one with the shiner — and do you know what she said? 'Blow the other little girls and boys! I want a pony, and I want it now!' I ask you, Bryant, what hope do we have for the future generation if they're all like this?'

Dick shuffled his papers. 'It's the result of the war, I imagine. Not that those kiddies will remember much about it, if they were even born back then. But their parents must have gone through all those years of rationing and shortages, and now they want to give their children everything they missed. It's only natural, I suppose. Oh, well, you haven't signed on for life, have you? Nobody's forcing you to go back on the job.'

'Only my wife,' Fry said glumly. 'Marie has her mind set on an Aga cooker and kitchen units and fancy tiles around the sink, the whole deal; and if the price of that is an occasional pair of wet pants, so what? 'You went all through the war with no complaints,' she says, 'so surely you can put up with a few lively youngsters?' Lively? I'll give 'em lively!'

★ ★ ★

'Poor old Fry,' Dick said that evening as he sat by his own fireside, recounting the events of his day to Maudie. 'I hope we bring up our Charlie to have more respect than that.'

'I can't recall seeing Father Christmas in the shops when I was young,' she said.

'As far as I recall, he stayed up at the North Pole, where he belonged, and we sent notes up the chimney to him, asking for what we hoped to get.'

'And did you? Receive what you asked for, I mean.'

'Not that I remember. My parents didn't have the money for bicycles and ballet slippers, although we had no idea that any gifts that came our way were bought by them. We always had some nuts and an orange in our stockings, though; perhaps a new jumper, knitted by Gran; and, if we were lucky, an annual of some sort. I did love those books! Christmas wouldn't have been Christmas without them.'

'I found a catapult in my stocking one year,' Dick remembered. 'I thought it was my best present ever.'

'I hope you didn't go round shooting poor cats and dogs,' Maudie said severely.

'Oh, no, but I did manage to give old Mrs Warrington a wallop, though.'

'What!'

'Well, it was an opportunity too good to miss. She was in the graveyard, bending over to tidy a grave, and her tweed-covered bottom was the perfect target. It was only a little pebble, but she leapt up screaming 'I've been shot! I've been shot!', and I suddenly realized the enormity of what I'd done.'

'It's a wonder they let you in the police force with a crime like that on your slate,' Maudie said.

'Oh, I shinned up a leafy tree and stayed there until the hue and cry died down. They never did find out who had shot Mrs Warrington, luckily for me, or my dad would have had his belt off in no time flat!'

'Boys will be boys,' Maudie said, laughing.

'Tell that to old Sarge Fry!'

'I can tell you one chap who deserves shooting, though, and that's that relief bus driver I came across today.' She went on to share her own unpleasant experience, while her husband listened gravely.

After leaving the clinic that morning, she had headed for the bus stop, eager to get home. Her earlier plan to visit Bentham's, where she could enjoy a cup of tea and a custard slice before having a look at the cosmetics counter, had been abandoned because the baby was becoming fractious again. The sooner he could be given a feed and put down in his cot, the better.

It was with some relief that she saw the green local bus arriving, right on time.

'You're not coming on board with that thing!' the driver told her, staring at the pushchair which she had somehow managed to fold up while balancing the wailing Charlie on her hip.

'What do you mean? And where's Bill Todd?' Their usual genial driver would never have spoken to her like that!

'Flu or summat. Like I said, you can't clutter up the bus with a great object like that.'

'Then put it in the luggage hold, please.'

'That's meant for suitcases and that. Now, are you getting on, or not? There's people waiting and you're holding up the queue.'

'And what am I supposed to do with my pushchair?'

18

He shrugged. 'Not my problem, lady.'

Maudie dithered for a moment. Dick was working, and she couldn't expect him to drop everything to drive them home. Neither could she abandon Charlie's pushchair. Her only option was to brazen it out.

'Out of my way!' she snapped, somehow managing to board the bus with baby, pushchair and all. She dragged the chair with her to a vacant seat, unwilling to risk having it thrown off the bus if she left it in the baggage cubbyhole.

The outraged tones of the substitute driver came to her ears. ''Ere! You can't do that!'

'I just did,' she said sweetly.

'I'll call the cops!' he threatened.

'Please do! My husband is a Detective Sergeant, and I'm sure he'll be happy to take down details of your complaint.'

Someone started to clap, quickly joined by the other passengers. 'Good for you, missus!' someone called, while Maudie sank back in her seat, settling Charlie more comfortably on her lap.

'Little Hitler!' she mumbled. 'Thinks

he can push people around, does he? We'll show him where to get off, won't we, little one?' The baby gurgled in response.

3

Greedy children aside, the Bryants were greatly looking forward to the fast-approaching magical Yuletide festival. For one thing, it would be their son's first Christmas, and although he wasn't old enough to take much notice, his parents would take delight in his presence as they celebrated the special season.

Maudie had already picked out a number of gifts at Bentham's that had been set aside under their popular layaway plan. She had put down a deposit to which she had added a few more shillings each week. Dick had grumbled about having to go in each week to pay in this modest amount, saying he could quite well afford to pay cash down and bring the items home right away, but she would have none of it. She had been brought up to be thrifty; and besides, her present to Dick was among the items reserved. He couldn't be allowed to pay for that!

She had considered long and hard what to buy for him. None of the ties on display seemed quite right, and socks and aftershave were too mundane. She hesitated over a pair of leather driving gloves, wincing at the price before giving up the idea. Dick was worth it, of course, but still . . . no need to mortgage the cottage just yet! She finally settled on a crimson lambswool scarf that would cheer up his sombre grey mackintosh. It was Christmassy enough, and would keep him warm through the frosty days of January and February; and if it turned out that he didn't like it after all, well, she could wear it herself!

For Charlie, she had chosen the most wonderful little wooden duck on wheels. When you pulled it along by a cord it flapped its wings and gave vent to a mechanical quacking sound. When she'd come upon a shop assistant demonstrating its charms to a gaggle of shoppers she had been unable to resist it.

'He's a bit young for anything like that, isn't he?' Dick had asked when Maudie had mentioned it. 'He's only four months old, love. Better wait until he's walking before we start buying pull toys.'

But nothing could quench her enthusiasm. The duck would keep, wouldn't it? And she happened to know that her lovely husband was secretly buying bits and pieces of miniature rolling stock to add to a train set, hiding them away in a trunk in the attic. Dick had cherished the train set of his boyhood until a few years ago, when he had given it to a sad little boy whose refugee parents were camping out in a disused railway carriage, having nowhere else to live.

At the time, Dick had believed that his chance of fatherhood had passed him by. He could not have foreseen that at the age of forty-five he would be presented with a tiny edition of himself by the woman he had fallen in love with and married in middle age. Now they had a little boy who could be introduced to the joys of model railroading by a doting father; at least, that was how Dick explained his motives to himself.

Smiling tolerantly, Maudie had purchased a small red signal box in secret, having looked through his little cache of treasures to make sure he didn't already have one. And a small clump of trees, made out of lead and painted green, also caught her eye. Well, the passengers had to have some nice scenery to look out at, didn't they? If she wasn't careful, they would both soon be playing trains as a hobby, whether young Charlie was interested or not!

After great deliberation, Maudie had settled on a turkey for their Christmas feast.

'Better not order too big a one,' Dick warned her.

'Why? You like turkey, don't you?'

'You know I do, love, but we don't want to be eating leftovers until Twelfth Night, do we?'

But that was precisely what Maudie did want. After the privations of the recent war, she relished the idea of a week filled with treats, and said so. Rissoles, shepherd's pie, creamed turkey; the possibilities were endless. She could imagine the aromas that would fill her kitchen as she worked.

'And don't forget hot turkey sandwiches,' Dick said, entering into the spirit of the thing. 'When I was in Canada, every restaurant had hot chicken or turkey sandwiches on the menu.'

'Oh, yes?' Maudie frowned. 'How did they work that, then? Surely they couldn't keep roasting one bird after another, just to have hot meat for sandwiches. What if not enough people ordered them? Think what a waste that would be!'

Dick grinned. 'Not at all! It's called a hot sandwich because it's smothered in gravy, and served with peas and French fries and coleslaw. Yummy! I wish you'd try it, Maudie. My mouth is watering at the very thought!'

'I'll add it to my list,' she assured him. It did sound good, although rather fattening if you had it too often!

There was still so much to do. Cards had to be written and sent off to friends far and near. Maudie was determined not to forget anyone. To her way of thinking, there was nothing worse than opening a card that the postman had delivered on

Christmas morning, only to find that it was from someone they'd forgotten or hadn't expected to receive greetings from. What did you do then? It was too late to reciprocate, but the card had to be acknowledged in some way. Would she have to pretend that she'd been too busy with the baby to finish the job this year?

'You worry too much, old girl,' Dick told her. 'And you know that half the cards we get come from your patients. They're a gesture of goodwill in recognition of your past services to them. People don't expect you to respond to those.'

'It's easy to see that you never lived in a small community like Llandyfan before you met me,' Maudie reminded him. 'Imagined slights have a habit of growing into full-blown feuds. Believe me, I know all about it.'

It sounded highly unlikely to Dick, but he held his peace.

* * *

If Maudie found it easy to find a gift that would delight her husband, that same man was at a loss when it came to reciprocating. He wanted to please his wife — but what did women really want? It was hard to know. They badly needed a new toaster: theirs was inclined to smoke at times, and it shot the toast into the air when you least expected it. However, he wouldn't like to see her face on Christmas morning if he presented her with a spanking new replacement. He knew her views on husbands who bought their wives something for the house, expecting grateful thanks!

Why not buy a toaster as a joke gift? Then, just when she was struggling to frame the right words, he would whip out the real present and they would have a good laugh. The problem was knowing what the real gift should be. He decided to have a word with his boss on the subject.

'You're a married man,' he began. DI Goodman frowned.

'For my sins.'

'Yes, well, I've got this problem, sir.'

'And what might that be, then?'

Dick plunged on. 'I don't know what to

get my wife for Christmas. I'd like to get her something really nice, only money's a bit tight, what with our mortgage and all'

'Have you asked her? Talk to her, man, that's my advice.'

'Yes, but that would spoil the surprise. Come on, sir, can't you give me some idea? And please don't say a frilly new nightie. I'm not going into the lingerie department at Bentham's and have everyone looking at me.'

'Scent,' Goodman said. 'You can't go wrong with that. Only none of your Woolworth's stuff, mind. It has to be a name brand, like Chanel or something.'

'I see. Thank you, sir. I'll think about what you've said.' Dick couldn't see what was wrong with the perfumes that Woolworth's sold: Maudie occasionally dabbed herself with *Evening in Paris* or *Californian Poppy*, and very nice they smelled, too. Still, the chief's wife was known to be a very stylish lady, so perhaps the chap knew what he was talking about.

Dick duly presented himself at the perfume counter at Bentham's, where he was faced with a bewildering array of bottles and atomizers. How on earth would he know what to choose?

'Can I help you, sir?'

With relief, he turned to face the motherly woman in her black dress who had offered to help. Thank goodness it wasn't one of those young girls who would make him feel a fool for dithering, but of course they were too busy gossiping to each other to deal with a homely-looking middle-aged man!

'I want to buy some perfume, please. For my wife,' he added, just in case the assistant got the idea he was shopping for a fancy woman.

'Yes, sir. Did you have any particular fragrance in mind? Lily of the valley is very nice, or lavender water is always acceptable.'

But Dick remembered his old Aunt Millie, who had always doused herself in lavender water. That was for old ladies, surely? He pointed to a small bottle standing on a red velvet-covered pedestal. 'How much is that one?'

'A very good choice, sir,' she told him,

reaching under the counter to retrieve a similar bottle in an attractive cardboard box.

Dick squawked in alarm when she mentioned the price. 'Good grief! Our monthly mortgage payment is less than that! Haven't you anything more, um . . . ?' He didn't want to say *cheaper*. Fortunately she understood.

'There is always the Eau de Toilette' she told him. 'You get the same fragrance for a fraction of the price. Many ladies prefer something lighter for everyday wear.'

But that didn't seem quite right to Dick, who had a smattering of French, learned while serving in the war. It made him think of the water that flowed out of the tank when you flushed the lavatory. 'I'll think about it and come back later,' he babbled.

The saleslady sighed and returned the little box to its hiding place under the counter. Roll on Christmas Eve, when the madness would be over and she could go home and soak her aching feet in a bowl of hot water with plenty of mustard in it.

Dick wandered off, buffeted by anxious shoppers and tired housewives. This shopping lark was no joke. Give him a decent crime to solve any day!

4

Somewhere a bell was clanging. Maudie was back in her old training hospital, having been assigned to work on Casualty. An ambulance was coming, bringing with it unmentionable horrors for them to deal with.

Matron appeared at her side, a forbidding expression on her face. 'You'll be sorry you've decided to come back to work, Nurse! It's been like Paddy's market here all night long, and now there's been a big accident on the ring road.' Matron's fingers were on Maudie's shoulder now, digging into the flesh.

'Gerroff!' Maudie howled, writhing in the woman's grasp. 'I didn't ask for this! I resign!'

'Come on, old girl, shake a leg! It's a quarter to seven. Didn't you hear the alarm?'

'Dick, is that you?'

'Of course it's me! Who did you think it

was, Father Christmas?'

She struggled to sit up. Had she actually slept all night, undisturbed? How marvellous it was to feel really rested! Then it dawned on her why that was. Charlie! Why hadn't he roused her? What was the matter with him? She shot out of bed and raced into the nursery, her heart thumping in her chest.

She found the baby studying his little hand as if he'd discovered it for the first time. He flexed his tiny fingers and chuckled. She put a hand on the cot rail to steady herself against the wave of nausea that swept over her momentarily.

'Kettle's boiling!' Dick called from the foot of the stairs. 'Shall I wet the pot?'

'Just coming!' Maudie left her son to his own devices and went to join her husband.

'Are you feeling all right, old girl? You're white as a sheet.'

'I was afraid Charlie had had a cot death,' she told him, and promptly burst into tears.

Dick took her into his arms, murmuring soothing noises. 'What on earth gave you an idea like that?'

'Because he didn't wake up in the night when he's been so fussy for weeks. I thought something must have happened to him.'

'Oh, he woke up at three o'clock, the same as usual, but you were dead to the world. I thought you needed a break after the rough time our son and heir has been giving you, so I took him for a little drive in the car and it seemed to calm him. He fell asleep as soon as I put him down again.'

'Oh, Dick! I just can't thank you enough!'

He grinned. 'Bacon and fried bread might do it!'

★   ★   ★

Greatly refreshed after her restful night, Maudie took Charlie and Rover for a walk later that morning, ending up at the vicarage. She found her friend polishing the communion silver with unusual vigour.

'There are times,' Joan Blunt muttered,

'when I regret that we live in a democracy!'

Maudie laughed. 'That doesn't sound like you! What's the trouble: more infighting among the Mothers' Union ladies?'

'If only it were so simple! No, there's a storm brewing over the celebration of Christmas in Llandyfan!'

'Surely the vicar has that all sewn up? The carol service on Christmas Eve, Midnight Mass later that night, and Matins on Christmas morning.'

'Yes, of course, but the problem is the nativity play.'

'But why? They always have that at the school, don't they? Or at least that's how it's been as long as I've been here.'

Joan Blunt sighed. 'The school hall is really much too small to accommodate all the parents and well-wishers, and now the headmistress has suggested using the parish hall instead. Harold doesn't mind; the school is Church of England, after all, so why shouldn't they use the facilities here? But one of the churchwardens says that if that's the case, then why don't they go the whole hog and have the play in the church?'

'Oh, I see. And perhaps the vicar doesn't feel comfortable with that?'

'He's torn two ways, poor man. He thinks it would destroy the holy atmosphere of the carol service to have all the upheaval of a school play happening right in front of the altar. It's not as if we have a stage in the church, and the children waiting their turn to appear would have to stand in the vestry, which is small and cramped. How on earth would the teachers manage to keep the little ones quiet, Nurse? You've helped with school plays, and you must recall the mayhem that goes on backstage.'

Maudie grinned. 'I know what you mean! *Miss, Johnny Davies sat on my crown and it's all squashed! Miss, my knicker elastic's busted! Miss, I think I'm gonna be sick!* Floods of tears all round.'

'Exactly.'

'If I were you, I'd have a quiet word with the headmistress. Possibly the presentation could be done without words? What I mean is, could the children be lined up outside and marched in at some appropriate moment in the carol service? You know the sort of thing: the three wise men arrive during the singing of *We Three Kings of Orient Are*. They quietly take their places in pews reserved for them, and whoever is doing the reading gives that part from the gospel.'

'It could work,' Mrs Blunt admitted. 'It would certainly save a lot of effort on the part of the teaching staff if there were no lines for the children to learn. Somebody always gets stage fright and dries up on the night! I'll go and have a word with Miss Rice and see if she can be persuaded. Thank you, Nurse! I feel sure that Harold will accept your idea as a good compromise.'

★ ★ ★

'And that was how we left it,' Maudie told Dick that evening, when they were sitting down to their evening meal of shepherd's pie and runner beans that Maudie had salted down in the autumn, watched closely by Rover, whose nose was trembling in anticipation. 'Aren't I a clever girl?'

Dick rolled his eyes. 'Just don't get too complacent, Maudie Bryant! Remember what the poet said about the best laid plans of mice and men.'

His wife shrugged. 'Not my problem. Like the wise woman I am, I've presented them with a sensible compromise and now my work is done. What they do with it is none of my business. It's up to the churchwardens and the Mothers' Union now.'

'That's what I'm afraid of,' Dick told her.

'Don't be such a gloomy guts. Do eat up. There's jam roly-poly and custard to follow!'

'I thought you said I ought to think of my waistline,' Dick grumbled, patting the part in question. 'There must be a million calories in a single helping of that!'

Maudie grinned. 'Well, if you don't want any, I'm sure Rover will mop up the leftovers!'

'I didn't say I didn't want it; and now I come to think of it, that dog is getting too heavy for his own good. I'll have a small portion and no second helping.'

'I know you, Dick Bryant,' Maudie warned. 'Don't even think about sneaking into the larder later on to see what you can find. I shall put the rest of the pudding out for the birds, all in the name of your svelte figure. See what a good little wife I am?'

'Which reminds me. I hope you can avoid getting mixed up in anything this holiday season.'

'What on earth are you talking about?'

'Murder! Arson! As long as I've known you, you've been mixed up in some sort of mayhem. Why, that's how we met, when you came across that body on the right of way above Oliver Bassett's farm. Since then, you've chalked up a body a year, and it's got to stop.'

'You make me sound like Jack the Ripper,' Maudie protested. 'It's hardly my fault if awful things keep happening.'

'No, but when they do, you should keep your nose out of the investigations and leave the detective work to the professionals. You are a wife and mother now. Your job is to sort out any problems that crop up on the home front, such as inventing a recipe for a delicious roly-poly that won't put extra inches on your hubby's tum! But what am I talking about? Things are pretty quiet now, and I really think we can look forward to a peaceful Christmas at home.'

'And so say all of us,' Maudie murmured, scraping leftovers into Rover's dish.

5

'Shall I pack a sandwich for your lunch?' Maudie asked, frowning at what was left of the cheese on the shelf. 'I could do cheese and pickle if you don't mind having more pickle than cheese.'

'Not today, thanks, love. The boys are going out for a pub lunch to celebrate the season. All the criminals seem to have taken a break for the moment, so we may as well enjoy the lull.'

Dick spoke too soon. As if in response to his optimistic words, the telephone rang shrilly, causing Rover to bark a warning. Charlie let out an anguished wail and waved his little arms about in distress.

'Hush, baby. Nothing's wrong.' Maudie jiggled the pram and the baby sank back into sleep. She tried to make out what Dick was saying, but his terse responses gave no clue to what was happening except that the call was obviously work-related.

'Sorry, love, got to go.' Dick hung up the phone and shrugged into his jacket.

'Wait a minute, Dick Bryant! Don't leave me in suspense! What's going on?'

'Murder!' he muttered, fumbling for his car keys. 'Somebody's bumped off Father Christmas.'

'What? Are you serious?'

'Never more so,' he said grimly, 'and I'm afraid it's our old sergeant who's been done in.'

'Not John Fry?' Maudie gasped. She knew the man well from Dick's earlier days at the Midvale police station. Dick didn't reply, but she could see by his expression that he feared the worst.

When his car had roared off, she poured herself another cup of tea and sat down to think. Who would want to kill poor John Fry, a kindly man who had come out of a peaceful retirement to make the season special for the local kiddies? Of course, much depended on where the assault had taken place. Perhaps he had been on his way home from Bentham's when he had run afoul of a gang of yobbos who thought it funny to beat up a universally loved symbol of Christmas, egging each other on until they went too far.

'Wait a minute, though,' she said aloud, causing Rover to raise his shaggy head from the hearthrug. 'Why would Sergeant Fry be walking home in his costume?' According to Dick, the man was embarrassed about his role, and usually travelled home by bus in plain clothes. He had said something about trying to hide wet trousers after an encounter with a nervous toddler.

She switched on the wireless, hoping to hear a news bulletin that would tell her more; but there was nothing but jolly music, obviously meant to cheer the housewife as she got down to scrubbing a floor or washing the breakfast dishes. That was no good; the media couldn't have got wind of the crime yet. Annoyed, she switched it off again.

It was all very well for Dick to tell her to mind her own business, but how could anyone hear about a murder without putting their wits to work? Of course she wouldn't put herself in harm's way — she was a mother now, after all — but if she happened to make some brilliant deduction, she would pass it on to Dick and let him take the credit for solving the crime. That was a wife's job, wasn't it? Bolstering her husband up and helping him to further his career.

★ ★ ★

Dick looked grey and anxious when he reached home that evening. His chin was covered with stubble and his tie was crooked.

'Get your coat off and come to the fire,' Maudie told him. 'I'll bring you a nice hot cup of tea.'

'Thanks, love. I could do with one.'

'Had a rough day, did you?' Maudie handed him a steaming cup. 'I've put extra sugar in. It looks to me like you could do with it.'

'Luckily, it wasn't as bad as I'd anticipated when the call first came in. To start with, it wasn't John Fry who got himself attacked. That's not to say that I don't care about the other poor bloke, but you know what I mean. The sarge is one of our own; or was, until he retired.'

'So who was the chap they killed?'

'Oh, he's not dead, thank the Lord. Unconscious in hospital with a nasty goose egg, but the doctors say he should come out of it, given time. His name is Alf Morton. Works for the Post Office, in the sorting office.'

'That's funny.'

'What's funny about that?'

'Well, it's almost Christmas, isn't it! This is the time of year when they take on extra staff to deal with the volume of mail. What was this chap doing dressed up as Father Christmas?'

Dick shrugged. 'Perhaps he was going to hand out presents to the kiddies at a party somewhere. We shan't know until he comes round.'

If he does come to, Maudie thought. Bumps on the head could do funny things to a person. The poor chap might have no memory at all of events leading up to the moment he was coshed.

★ ★ ★

The next day, Maudie packed Charlie into his pram and walked up to the village shop. She found Mrs Hatch, the owner and postmistress, avidly reading the latest edition of the Midvale Chronicle.

'I suppose you know all about this, Nurse, what with your hubby being a copper,' she said. 'Awful, isn't it? What are things coming to when it isn't safe for poor old Father Christmas to walk the streets in broad daylight?'

'It's too bad, all right, but why should he expect to be any safer than the average citizen? Little old ladies and young mothers with prams have just as much right to walk about without fear.'

Mrs Hatch looked at Maudie over the top of her spectacles. 'You don't understand, Nurse. Think of all the kiddies who really believe in Father Christmas. What are they going to think now? If he can be struck down, something nasty could happen to anybody.'

'It's a wicked world, Mrs Hatch.'

'You never said a truer word, Nurse. Just listen to this. 'Alfred Morton, sixty-two, employed by the GPO, was struck down in the street on Thursday by an unknown assailant. The perpetrators left him lying in a pool of his own blood when they fled the scene. It isn't known whether robbery was the motive.' Think of that, Nurse! A pool of his own blood! It's a wonder the poor man wasn't drowned!'

'I doubt if it was quite that bad,' Maude said, picking up a tin of peas and putting it down again. 'Don't you have these in a smaller size, Mrs Hatch? These are too much for two people, and there's not much you can do with leftover peas.'

'Put them in an omelette. That's what I'd do. And I do think you're hard, Nurse. I suppose that's what nursing does to you. You're so used to seeing sights that would turn a normal person's stomach, you don't care any more.'

'Oh, nurses do care, all right,' Maudie assured her. 'We just don't get rattled over every little thing, that's all. Now then, I'll take a couple of pound of carrots, please.'

With a sniff the older woman went to put the carrots on her scale. Maudie wandered over to a display of tinned peaches and put a can in her shopping basket. Pea omelette, indeed! She could just see Dick's face if she served up one of those. Rover would be the lucky recipient of an unexpected plate of people food, although most likely he would turn up his wet black nose at it as well.

'Just be sure you never do anything to get yourself into this ghastly newspaper,' Mrs Hatch said, placing the carrots in Maudie's basket and taking note of the tin of peaches as she went to the till.

'I'll try not to, but why, exactly?'

'See what it says here! 'Alfred Morton, sixty-two'! Why do they always have to put people's ages in the paper for all to see? Do you think I'd want everyone knowing my age? 'Vera Hatch, fifty-nine'? I'd just die of embarrassment!'

And everyone else would die laughing, because you're pushing seventy, if I'm any judge, Maudie thought; but she was too well brought up — and much too kind — to say it.

6

It wasn't long before it came out that Alf Morton had left the post office under a cloud.

'Much better for him if he never comes out of that comma,' Mrs Hatch muttered, when Maudie called in to buy a postal order to send to a godchild for Christmas.

'Coma,' Maudie corrected automatically.

'That's what I said, didn't I? He's lying there in one of them commas. Like as not he's faking it, see, to put off the evil day.'

'I'm sure the doctors would know the difference, Mrs Hatch.'

'That's as may be, but when he does come round it will be straight into jail for him, you mark my words. It says here he's been dismissed from his work, and charges are pending. What do you make of that, eh? Ah, you're expecting that little boy to get that money you're sending, aren't you, so he can buy himself a nice toy or something; but just think of all the people who won't never get what's rightfully theirs on account of that great lummox having pocketed the lot!'

'I agree it's a very bad thing that he's done, but surely the chap doesn't deserve to die because of it. It's not as if he's murdered anyone.'

'He's tampered with His Majesty's mail service, and we can't have that! And think of the disgrace his family will have to face. I feel sorry for his poor wife, if he's got one.'

Maudie knew from what Dick had let slip that the whole sorting department was under suspicion. There was some indication that thefts had been going on for some time, and the problem was too widespread for it to have been done by one man alone.

What if this Morton was an innocent victim of others who were behind the crime? Possibly he had discovered what was going on and threatened to expose those involved. The attack on him could have been a warning to keep his nose out of other people's affairs, or even an attempted murder that failed. She would mention this theory to Dick in case he hadn't thought of it himself.

It was a warm day for December, so she decided to take the long way round on the way home, to give Charlie an airing and let Rover stretch his legs. This took her past the village school, and as soon as she came within sight of the place she knew that something was going on. The playground was in an uproar and a young teacher, who Maudie hadn't met before, seemed to be in some difficulty.

Putting the brake on the pram, Maudie sailed in to help. 'I'm Nurse Bryant. Can I help in any way?'

'I'm Gwyneth Probert,' the young woman responded. The lilt of the Welsh valleys was musical on her tongue. 'It's these attacks on Father Christmas, you see. It's upset the children very much, and there seems to be nothing I can do to make it right.' The girl seemed close to tears.

Maudie held up a hand for silence, and the chattering ceased.

'Now then, you lot! You know me,

don't you? Nurse Bryant.' There were nods and tentative smiles. After all, she had ushered most of these youngsters into the world, so she was an old friend.

'What's going on here, then? No, don't all talk at once! You there — Bobby Fleming. Can you tell me what the matter is?'

'This lot's crying 'cause Father Christmas got bashed on the head,' he said. 'What a lot of babies! Everyone knows there's no such thing as Father Christmas!'

'There is so, you fibber! And if he dies, we won't get no presents for Christmas, so there!'

Bobby turned on the little girl who had interrupted. 'Don't be so silly. It's your mum and dad what brings you presents. Don't you know anything?'

The child flew at Bobby, pounding on his chest with tiny fists.

'Here, that's enough of that,' Maudie said, separating the two. 'Now, you listen to me. To start with, the man who was attacked isn't dead.'

'Yes he is, Miss! It says so in the

Chronicle. My dad read it out to us at breakfast.'

'Then the *Chronicle* is wrong. That poor man is in hospital, and I know that because my husband told me so. He's a detective, you see. And that man isn't Father Christmas, he was just somebody dressed in a costume. The real Father Christmas is at home in the North Pole, making sure the elves get everything ready for delivery on Christmas Eve.'

'What was that man dressed up for, then?' a tiny boy asked. Maudie could see that his sleeve was all wet. No doubt he'd been chewing on it in his anxiety.

'Well,' Maudie said, fumbling for the right words, 'everybody dresses up at Christmas, don't they? I expect some of you will be in the nativity play, dressed as shepherds or the three wise men. Everybody knows you're not the real shepherds and kings, but just children playing a part. The real shepherds are ... ' She hesitated. Better not say they'd been dead for nineteen hundred years, and set this lot off again! 'They're in the Bible,' she finished.

'And this afternoon we're going to read all about it,' Miss Probert said. 'It's time to go in now. Form lines, please. Take your distance! No pushing and shoving there, you boys!'

Maudie retreated, happy to let the everyday business of the school resume. Phew! Dealing with young children was no joke! Who knew what muddles their little minds got into at times? And she had all that to come in the future with young Charlie!

* * *

That evening, she explained her theory to Dick, who grinned at her. 'Thanks, love. Of course we thick-headed coppers would never have thought of that!'

'But you've got to admit it's a possibility, Dick!'

'Not any more. We were able to get a search warrant for Morton's flat, and we found enough evidence to send him down for a long time.'

'What sort of evidence?'

'A pile of postal orders, for a start, and

a cash box with quite a few ten-bob notes in it; more money than he could have raked in from honest work, even if he did put in extra hours at Bentham's. It seems that he'd been helping himself to anything he comes across in the post that looked as if it might contain money. Why people put cash in the post, I don't know. They might know it's an open invitation to thieves.'

'Postal orders aren't safe either, by the sound of it! And to think I bought one today to send to little Julian. I shan't know what to do with it now.'

'It should be safe enough now the gang have been rumbled,' Dick observed.

'The gang? Do you mean there's more than one person involved in the thefts?'

Dick tapped the side of his nose. 'I've said too much already! Now then, what's for tea? This detective business makes a man hungry!'

★ ★ ★

Two days later, the *Chronicle* reported that man in the hospital had come round from his coma to find the police waiting to speak to him.

''My mind is a complete blank,' Alfred Morton told our reporter on Friday.'

'I bet it is!' Maudie muttered on reading this.

''All I can remember is leaving a children's party where I had been hired to hand out parcels, and I must have been on my way home, but after that, nothing at all until I woke up to find myself in hospital. When I felt the bump on my head I thought I must have been run over, but they tell me I was attacked, and I can't think why. It's not as if I was carrying a lot of cash with me. All I had on me was the ten bob they paid me to do the job. What's the world coming to if even poor old Father Christmas isn't safe from muggers?''

'Quite a sob story,' Maudie muttered, having no sympathy for a man who had robbed customers of similar amounts — or often much less — entrusted to the Royal Mail. Pensioners sending a painfully saved half-crown to a grandchild, perhaps; or honest citizens like herself sending a few shillings to a small godchild. Why, given the chance, she might have walloped the beastly man over the head herself! Since she hadn't been given that opportunity, she hoped he'd end up serving a very long prison term, once the police got around to charging him with his crimes.

7

It might be December, but that was no excuse for sitting at home putting on weight, Maudie decided. Besides, when Christmas came, there would be temptation on all sides in the shape of gravy and puddings, chocolates and Christmas cake! You could say one thing for the recent war, there was no chance of anybody getting fat while food was so stringently rationed. Nowadays, one was only too likely to indulge, if only because one recalled those days of austerity.

Charlie was almost five months old now, and Maudie hadn't yet regained her sylph-like figure. (*And who am I kidding?* she reproved herself. Those were words that could never have been applied to her. 'Pleasingly plump', perhaps?) So, on fine days, she packed the baby into his pram, warmly dressed with just his little red cheeks showing, tied Rover's lead to the handle, and set off to get some exercise.

And if, on returning home, she felt the need of a hot cup of tea with something delectable to go with it — well, it was the thought that counted, wasn't it? A good brisk walk in the cold air must have worn off a few calories, surely?

On one such expedition, Maudie came across a woman sitting on the stile beside a field that was part of the estate belonging to Cora Beasley, the owner of the local big house. Although she appeared to be warmly dressed for the weather, she was hunched over as if in pain. Maudie's nursing instincts came to the fore, and she moved forward to stop beside the woman.

'Excuse me! Are you feeling ill? Can I help you at all? I'm a nurse.'

The woman's head came up slowly. 'I'm quite all right, thank you, madam.'

Madam? That didn't sound like anyone Maudie knew. Everyone within a five-mile radius usually addressed her as Nurse, even though, strictly speaking, she was no longer practicing her profession.

The woman's gaze turned to Charlie in his pram. 'That's a baby!' she muttered.

'You take my advice, madam, and don't you never get yourself one of those!'

'It's a bit late for that now,' Maudie told her. Was the woman perhaps mentally ill? She must prepare herself to defend Charlie if the poor soul made a sudden move.

'This is my little boy,' she murmured. 'Perhaps you've lost a baby of your own?'

'You could say that.' The woman's tired blue eyes seemed filled with grief. 'Lily Rose, her name was. Still is, if she's still alive. My husband named her that. 'I am the rose of Sharon, and the lily of the valleys.' That's in the Bible, you know. The Song of Solomon.'

'Yes, that's right. How old is your little girl?'

'Just seventeen.'

'And she isn't with you now?'

'My husband put her out. That's what comes of having children, you see, madam. You do your best to bring them up in the way they should go, and then they bring shame and disgrace on you. Oh, you may not believe me now, with that little boy sitting in his pram with the face of a little angel; but your turn is bound to come and there's nothing you can say or do to prevent it.'

Midwife Maudie thought she understood. This woman's daughter had found herself to be in trouble, and the husband had come the outraged father and shown the girl the door. Despite it being 1951, there were still men who behaved like actors in a Victorian melodrama. Having a child out of wedlock still brought shame on a family, and for many it was thought to be a sin as well.

Others accepted it philosophically. Maudie had brought several babies into the world who were now being brought up as the youngest sibling of their aunts and uncles, some of whom were close in age to the newborn itself.

This woman obviously needed help, so plain speaking shouldn't come amiss. 'I assume you're saying that your Lily Rose is in trouble, and that's why your husband made her leave home? Have you any idea where she is?'

The woman stared at her. 'If I knew that, I'd bring her back, no matter how much Ivan ranted and raved. It's not knowing that's driving me wild, can't you see? The girl must be close to her time, but is there anyone to help her? For all I know, she has no place to lay her head!'

'Is it possible she's gone to the father of her child? Perhaps his people have taken her in?'

The woman's mouth twisted. 'She says he was one of them labourers, a young man who came with the builders when we were having the church roof put right. 'He told me he loved me,' she kept saying, when her dad wrung it out of her who had brought her so low. Of course she didn't know anything, poor girl. That was her dad's wish, you see, his way of keeping her pure. She didn't know the ways of the world.'

'Or of young men in particular,' Maudie said grimly. 'I don't think I know your Lily Rose, Mrs . . . er . . . ?'

'Croome. Mrs Ivan Croome.'

'You're not from these parts, I take it?'

'We live the other side of Brookfield.'

'Then you're a few miles from home, if you don't mind my saying so.'

'I've come to see that Mrs Beasley. My hubby works for her on a farm she owns on the Brookfield road. I was hoping that if she heard my story she might have a word with him; threaten him, like, say she'd sack him if he didn't let me search for our Lily Rose before it's too late. Only once I'd got this far, my heart failed me, and I was afeard to go on. What if she hears my tale and sacks him anyway, out of principle, like? Then we'd be with no money coming in and my hubby not speaking to me, and Lily Rose still goodness knows where!'

'It's a problem all right,' Maudie agreed. 'Look, I know Cora Beasley quite well; how would it be if I had a word with her about all this? And my husband is a police detective who knows how to find missing persons. Let me have the details, and I'll get him working on this right away.'

Mrs Croome leapt up in alarm. 'Oh, not the police! Dear me, no! Ivan would never forgive me! I've said too much already. Let it go, for the love of heaven!' She hobbled off down the road, and the last Maudie saw of her was her agitated figure rounding the corner by the ancient chestnut tree where generations of local boys had found their conkers.

'You handled that really well, Maudie Bryant!' Annoyed with herself, Maudie bit her lip.

'Arf!' sighed Rover, who was aching to be off.

⋆　⋆　⋆

That evening, Maudie told Dick about her encounter in the hope that he might do something to help the distraught mother.

'From what you say, it doesn't sound as if the girl has been reported as a missing person,' he said. 'That being the case, there doesn't seem to be much we can do. It sounds more like a job for the Salvation Army. We just don't have the manpower to look into things which are really none of our concern.'

'But that poor woman, Dick! She's half out of her mind with worry, as any mother would be.'

'I sympathize, old girl; of course I do. But things may not be as bad as the mother believes. The girl may have gone to an aunt, say, or a grandmother.'

'Not as far as this Mrs Croome knows. Obviously she's done the round of the relatives to see if anyone knows anything.'

'Then what about those places where they take in unwed mothers-to-be? If you come across this woman again, you might suggest that. If she's found her way to such a home, that could explain why she's dropped off the radar.'

'Or she could be lying in a ditch somewhere, murdered, or dead from exposure!'

'In which case the death would come to our attention, sooner or later.'

'Dick Bryant! How can you be so hard-hearted?'

He shrugged. 'I'm only saying, old girl, that's all.'

8

'And I can't sop thinking about that poor girl,' Maudie concluded, having told her story to Joan Blunt. 'Being pregnant is difficult enough, without being homeless in this sort of weather.' The rain was lashing down outside, and there seemed little chance of Llandyfan seeing a traditional white Christmas.

'I expect she's holed up in a squat somewhere with other young people,' the vicar's wife said. 'There are still plenty of bombed-out buildings left, especially in the cities. It's her mother I feel sorry for. She not only has the worry of her daughter's disappearance, but also has to live with that unforgiving man she's married to. So what if the girl has taken a wrong turning? She isn't the first, and she certainly won't be the last. Whatever happened to Christian forgiveness?'

'Mr Blunt must know the vicar at Brookfield. Couldn't he put in a word for the Croomes? At least prevail upon the father to let his wife trace the girl, even if he won't let her come home? I'm sure it would ease the poor woman's mind if she knew Lily Rose is in some sort of shelter for expectant mums.'

'I shall certainly speak to Harold about this, Nurse, but the Croomes may not be Church of England. I seem to recall hearing about a rather strict religious sect that has sprung up on the outskirts of Brookfield. You know the sort of thing. Anything joyful is bound to be a sin. Christmas is a pagan festival and shouldn't be encouraged.'

'How can Christmas be a pagan festival?' Maudie asked.

'Apparently, the early Christian missionaries felt it would be asking too much to make people give up their celebrations connected with their old gods, so they superimposed the festival of Christ's birth onto the old Winter Solstice.

'When I was a girl, we had a poor child in our class whose parents belonged to such a sect. She wasn't allowed to take part in the nativity play, and when the teacher asked her why, the child said that Jesus wasn't born in December because the shepherds wouldn't have been out in the fields with their sheep then, and a lot more besides. At that age, the theological argument escaped me, but I remember being horrified when I heard that poor Mildred wouldn't have any Christmas presents.'

'That's it!' Maudie yelped, causing Charlie to flinch on her lap. She rubbed his little back and he sank back into sleep with a tiny yawn.

'I beg your pardon?'

'Oh, don't mind me, Mrs Blunt! It's just this business of the attack on Father Christmas, you see. The newspaper reports have got everyone worried, even the little ones up at the school.

What if it has to do with that sect at Brookfield? They don't hold with Christmas and they want to strike out at something. Poor old Father Christmas is a symbol; an instrument of the devil, as far as they are concerned.'

Mrs Blunt scratched her chin thoughtfully. 'I don't know about that, Nurse! I can see they might have strong feelings on the subject, although we really don't know what their views are in that direction, but murder? That would be a step too far!'

'Somebody ought to attend one of their services and ask a few questions,' Maudie argued.

'Don't look at me, Nurse! Harold would have a fit if I did any such thing. I suggest you share your theory with Mr Bryant and let the proper authorities deal with it, if indeed there is anything to be dealt with. Besides, haven't you promised him you would steer clear of mayhem and murder now you're a mother?'

'Mm,' Maudie said. If it hadn't been for the fact that she needed both hands to hold her son safely on her lap, she might have crossed her fingers behind her back.

★　★　★

'It's certainly something we should look into,' Dick agreed, when Maudie told him her suspicions. 'How did you come to think of it, anyway?'

'Joan Blunt gave me the idea. I was

telling her about the missing girl and her unforgiving father, and she mentioned that religious sect.'

'And she knows for a fact that being against Christmas is one of their beliefs, does she?'

'Well, no, not exactly. But it shouldn't be too hard to find out.'

'We already know quite a bit about them, love, and they seem to be a law-abiding lot, as far as we know. They don't have a church or chapel as such; they recently took over an empty workshop on the edge of Brookfield, and that's where they hold their services. Their members also tend to go out and about holding impromptu services on street corners, reading the Bible aloud and singing hymns. All very dignified. We've had no complaints about them from the public.'

'Then why not go and have a word with their minister? Sound him out on his views about the trappings of the season?'

'Apparently they don't have a minister as such. The men of the church take it in turns to preach sermons and lead the singing and so on.'

'Couldn't we just . . . ' Maudie began.

Dick wagged a finger in front of her nose. 'If you're going to suggest that we drop in on one of their services, just to see what we can see; the answer is no, we could not! It's one thing for me to call there — on a weekday, mind — in the course of a police investigation, but quite another to attend a service out of morbid curiosity! Until proved otherwise, these are sincere people, worshipping according to their beliefs, even if those beliefs do seem strange to us. This is a free country, Maudie. Isn't that what we fought a war for?'

'Spoilsport!' Maudie muttered.

★ ★ ★

As it happened, Dick was unable to find anyone to interview during the days that followed. The meeting hall was pad-locked, and presumably the members were all at work during the day. He did, however, find a tattered notice pinned to the door, fluttering in the breeze, that

71

drew attention to a prayer meeting on the Wednesday evening.

Grumbling, Maudie remained at home with Charlie, feeling resentful. Having managed to get the baby settled in good time, she decided on an early night, and was soon tucked up in bed with a cup of Horlicks and a new library book. When she heard Dick's key in the door, however, she thrust her arms into her warm dressing gown and rushed down to interrogate him.

'What was it like? Did you find out anything?'

'Let me get inside the door, love! And I could do with a cup of something. It's perishing cold out there. That wind must be coming straight down from Russia!'

'Tea or cocoa? I've had Horlicks, but I used the last of it.'

'Better make it cocoa,' Dick said, attacking the remains of the living room fire with the poker. 'If I have tea, I'll be up all night.'

Maudie put the kettle on and foraged in the pantry for something to go with the cocoa. Only a piece of stale pound cake came to light, so she put two slices of bread under the grill. The aroma of toast was so enticing that she made two more pieces for herself, and added a pot of plum jam to the tray. She would give the crusts to Rover, so the calories she consumed would be negligible, wouldn't they? As for the dog, he was such an active animal that he never seemed to put on an excess pound.

Soon all three were enjoying their feast. 'Go on, then,' Maudie prompted. 'What was it like?'

'Not much to tell, really,' Dick mumbled through a slice of toast heavily laden with jam. 'There was nothing much inside the place other than a few rows of plain wooden chairs. No pulpit or anything.'

'Not even a piano?'

'No. The chap who led the singing had a tuning fork. I haven't seen one of those since I was a nipper. Oh, and the women sat on one side of the aisle, if you could call it that, and the men on the other. It was all quite decorous, really. One or two hymns, and the sort of sermon you might expect: all hellfire and brimstone. When it was all over, I introduced myself to the chap who gave the sermon; he convinced me that they're all pacifists, and murder or grievous bodily harm definitely runs contrary to their beliefs.'

'Well, he would say that, wouldn't he?'

'I thought he seemed sincere. And yes, I did ask if they celebrate Christmas; and was told that of course they accept that Christ was born into the world, but just not on the twenty-fifth of December. He suggested that the attack on Father Christmas was probably carried out by hooligans doing it for kicks, and my boss tends to agree. So, this turned out to be nothing but a wild goose chase, but that's police work all over. We keep following every avenue until one day we hit on something worthwhile.'

'But the missing girl! What about her?'

'I didn't get anywhere with that.'

'Oh, Dick!'

'I did put out a feeler, but the chap cut me off short, saying that their members reserve the right to discipline their young people as they see fit. 'Spare the rod and spoil the child', the Bible says.'

'You'd have done better to talk to the women. Surely some of them must feel a bit of sympathy for a pregnant teenager lost and alone somewhere. Well, it's not too late to find out. I wonder if these people have a women's sewing circle or something? Making little pairs of trousers to clothe the heathen abroad somewhere.'

'Maudie!'

'What?'

'Don't come the innocent with me, my girl. You are not to go rushing in where angels fear to tread! Do you hear me?'

'I hear you,' she said; but so what? She was a midwife and a mother of a young baby, and on both counts that gave her the right to feel concerned about a young woman at risk. 'Isn't it time we went up, Dick? Morning comes early, you know. Will you bank up the fire, or shall I?'

9

Maudie glanced at the clock for what must be the twentieth time since she'd laid the table for tea. It was past seven o'clock, and Charlie had already been put down in his cot. Dick had missed playing with the child in the bath, and now would not see him again until morning.

'Where on earth is that master of yours?' she demanded, frowning down at Rover who had already taken up his station under the table. 'It's not like him to be so late without phoning to let me know he'll be delayed. Luckily, it's lamb cutlets, and I can pop them under the grill when he gets here, but I shan't know when to start the potatoes. Well, there's no point in keeping you waiting, dog. Come and get your dinner, then.'

Rover sniffed at the dried food in his bowl and backed away, looking up at her accusingly. *What do you call this, then? I know you have chops waiting!* Maudie ignored his pleading and went to the window. The street outside was deserted. A persistent drizzle showed silver in the light cast by a nearby streetlamp. Tutting, she let the curtain fall. Surely he must come soon?

When the Whittington chimes of the clock on the sideboard announced that it was eight o'clock, she returned to the window. Her view was now obscured by a swirling mist. Something must have happened to Dick! A car smash, a terrible collision in the fog ... Dick transported to hospital. Herself a widow. Charlie growing up fatherless. She went to the phone, not at all reassured by the dial tone that greeted her. She put the receiver back in its cradle, swallowing a small sob.

It was well after nine when she heard the muffled sound of a car door slamming. Was it Dick at last, or one of her colleagues steeling himself to deliver bad news? She flew to the door and flung it open.

'Dick Bryant! Where have you been?' He opened his arms wide but she ignored the gesture, pummelling his chest with clenched fists.

'Steady on, old girl! You'll have me over!'

'Why didn't you call? I've been out of my mind with worry!'

'I'll tell you all about it later. Can you let me get this door shut? You're letting all the warmth out.'

Maudie backed away, trying to calm down. She had never got into a flap like this during her nursing days, no matter how serious the situation. She knew now that you became a hostage to fortune as soon as you fell in love. Fear stalked the back of one's mind whenever the possibility of loss loomed.

This was no time for dwelling on philosophy! She must get the chops on. 'Come to the fire,' she murmured, in control of herself again. 'Your meal won't be long.' She might as well forget about the potatoes. They could have bread and butter instead. The mint sauce was already made, and the peas were waiting in the pot.

'Charlie all right, is he?' Dick called

from the fireside.

'Oh, yes. He went off quite happily.'

'Good, good. Anything new and exciting happening here?'

'All quiet on the Western Front,' Maudie quoted, coming in to remove the cutlery from the dining table. In the circumstances, it seemed sensible to eat off trays in front of the fire on a night such as this.

'I'm sorry I didn't check in to let you know,' Dick said at last, when he had put away two helpings of stewed apples and custard. 'All hell broke loose at home time, and I was called out to deal with it.'

'Oh, yes?'

'There's been another attack on Father Christmas, and this time poor old Fry was the target.'

'No! Is he all right?'

'Tucked up in hospital with a broken clavicle, but he'll recover in time, the docs say.'

Maudie's thoughts went to Dick's former colleague, who had come through a lifetime of police work unscathed, only to be injured in a bizarre attack while trying to bring a little pleasure into the lives of young children. It just didn't seem fair.

'Wait a minute! Didn't he resign from that job at Bentham's?'

'That's right, but when his replacement finished up in hospital, he was asked to come back for the duration.'

'So what actually happened this time?'

'According to Fry, he was on his tea break, and on his way back to the grotto he stopped in at the staff gents'. He was just washing his hands when a chap armed with a cricket bat came in. Luckily, Fry caught a glimpse of him in the bit of mirror they have on the wall there, and he leapt aside in the nick of time. That's how he came to get his shoulder blade broken instead of taking the full brunt of the blow on his head.'

'Didn't the attacker have another go?'

'Luckily one of the stock boys happened to come in at the opportune moment.'

'Gave him the old one-two, did he? Our hero to the rescue?'

'Apparently he just stood there gawping. The boy was pushed aside and sent sprawling while the villain made his escape. It was Fry who sounded the alarm in the end.'

'Could either of them identify the man?'

'Not a chance. He was wearing a balaclava. I did ask the boy if he'd noticed the colour of the chap's eyes, but all he could say was that his eyes were 'glittering with menace'. I'd say that youth has been reading too many penny dreadfuls!'

'So I suppose you went to the cottage hospital with poor old Fry?'

'I did, and that's what held me up. Casualty was overflowing with a lot of accident victims, which wasn't surprising on a filthy night like this. The sarge spent ages propped up on a trolley with me sitting beside him, trying to keep his mind off his injuries. Of course the ambulance attendant had put his arm in a sling, so that was one blessing.'

'Everyone has been suggesting that the first Father Christmas was set upon by youths out for kicks,' Maudie mused. 'But this time it's different, isn't it? Only one fellow — as if that wasn't enough — and it does seem as though the attack was planned. Instead of hanging about in the streets where he might have been noticed, he zeroes in on Father Christmas's place of work. Good thinking, that, because the store must be teeming with customers at this time of year. Who would notice one more shopper in a woolly hat?'

'And I suspect that he picked up the weapon in the sports department on the off-chance. All right, so this isn't the cricket season, but Bentham's must keep a selection of bats in stock year-round. Acceptable Christmas gift for the enthusiast, sort of thing.'

'And then he sees Father Christmas going into the lavatory and follows him in, pulling the balaclava over his face as he goes. But why, Dick? Why target Father Christmas? Or is it a case of some maladjusted youth who still feels resentful that the old boy let him down years ago when he longed for a pair of football boots that never arrived?'

'Hardly. But while we were sitting there

in Casualty, old Fry did come up with the idea that perhaps he'd been the target all along, and the Father Christmas thing is just coincidence. The perpetrator is probably some crook, recently released from prison, who got sent down by Fry in the past. Now he's out for revenge. Morton, the first victim, was probably in the wrong place at the wrong time.'

'So now what?'

'So now we must catch this chap in the act, and after that we hope he'll come clean and we'll know what it was all about.'

'If he has any sense, he'll lie low after this, I should think.'

'Ah, but since when has the average criminal seen sense? No, I believe he'll have another go — and it will have to happen soon, because Christmas is almost here, and the old red suit and the false beard will be put into mothballs for another year.'

'But John Fry won't be able to return to work, will he? Not with a broken shoulder. And after all the publicity, you won't find another out-of-work granddad willing to come and take his chances at being flattened by a homicidal maniac.'

'True enough, love. That's why somebody from the department will have to go undercover.'

'Dick, no!' Maudie screeched. 'Please tell me you're not going to volunteer! It's too dangerous! Find somebody who's a judo expert or something.'

But even as she spoke, she knew that if Dick intended to put his life on the line there was nothing she could do to prevent it. This was the man who had saved a toddler from an enraged bull in Canada. When an arsonist had managed to set himself on fire, who had borne him to the ground, beating out the flames with only his overcoat to keep him from sustaining bad burns himself? Dick Bryant, the hero, that was who!

10

Maudie closed her front door quietly, leaving her husband and son behind. In her days as a single and professional woman, she would never have dreamed that the thought of attending a parish meeting could be so enticing. Now, when much of her day seemed to be taken up with feeding and changing baby Charlie, boiling nappies in a pail on top of the cooker, and trying to stay alert after yet another wakeful night, the prospect of an hour or two spent with other adults seemed like paradise regained.

'Off you go, love; I'll hold the fort,' Dick said while she stood dithering in the doorway. She hardly needed telling twice — yet would he know what to do if their baby was sick? Would he be able to distinguish between a cry of pain and just a loud complaint when Charlie didn't want to be left alone in his cot to go to sleep?

'Of course, if you'd rather not leave him, I'm sure people will understand,' Dick murmured, with low cunning. 'I'll go in your place, if you like. In fact, I think I ought to . . . '

'I'm going! I'm going!' Maudie scuttled away before she lost her chance of freedom. Their cottage was just a few yards away from the parish hall. If anything really did go wrong, Dick could reach her in minutes.

The meeting was already in progress when she tiptoed into the hall. Having sidled into the back row, she looked around cautiously, wondering what she had missed. Churchwarden Oliver Bassett was in the chair, officiously taking notes. The vicar sat beside him, and Maudie could tell from the pained expression on his face that something had displeased him.

'To recap,' Bassett said, 'this year it has been decided to hold the school nativity play here in the parish hall. This is the case for two reasons: the hall can accommodate a larger audience, and everyone can go from here to the carol service in the church, which will be convenient for those coming from a distance. Speaking for myself, I feel that this is the cause of some unnecessary duplication. The children have been allocated what I would term walk-on parts, presenting a sort of tableau while the appropriate passages of scripture are read. I'm sure this will be a disappointment to the parents who have come to see the youngsters in action. I must ask you now: is it possible to make a change for the better?'

Oh, dear! Maudie thought. *That has set the cat among the pigeons, and no mistake! And it's all my fault. Me and my bright ideas!*

All eyes turned to the headmistress of the village school when she rose to speak.

'This is all very well, Mr Chairman, but I must point out that it's far too late to change now! I don't think you understand how long it takes to get young children to learn their parts, or the time it takes away from regular classroom activities to drill them in their roles. Besides, they won't be exactly mute, you know!

The readings will be given by some of the older pupils, and everyone will join in the carols, of course.'

'And then we all goes into the church and sings them all over again,' someone called out. All heads swivelled towards the speaker, and back again to Miss Rice.

'Not necessarily. I'm sure the vicar has approved a most interesting selection of music and readings. Beside, it will be a wonderful experience for the children to process into the candlelit church and take part in an age-old service. Why, the organ music alone will be an inspiration to them. And I am pleased to announce that we have another treat in store. Our junior mistress, Miss Gwyneth Probert, has agreed to perform two solos of sacred music!' Miss Rice beamed at the assembled villagers, who glared back at her.

'Will she be singing here in the hall, then, or in church?'

'Oh, in the church, of course, at the carol service. Miss Probert has a beautiful soprano voice. Welsh, of course, and a treat to listen to.'

'Gladys Brown is our soloist,' someone muttered. 'Is she not to sing, then? She's never missed a Christmas service in forty years!'

'Miss Probert will be our *guest* soloist,' Joan Blunt told them, raising her voice to make herself heard above the hubbub. 'Naturally, Mrs Brown will have her part to play as usual. That goes without saying.'

Personally, Maudie thought that it was about time that Gladys Brown retired gracefully. Faithful she might be, but her voice was no longer what it had been in her youth. In fact, she now had trouble hitting the high notes. If Maudie had her way, poor Gladys would be presented with a lovely gift in honour of her years of service, given a round of applause, and relegated to the back row of the choir. She chided herself for the uncharitable thought.

'What about the animals?' someone called. 'Our Larry brought a note home saying you wanted toy lambs and that. We don't have none of them. Will a teddy bear do?'

'I'm afraid there were no bears in Bethlehem,' Miss Rice said firmly. 'Perhaps you could make a sheep costume for your little boy to wear instead?'

'Better make it a black one, then,' someone muttered. 'We all know what sort of mischief that Larry Thomson gets up to when he thinks nobody's looking.'

'You speak for yourself, Tom Crowe!' Larry's mother bawled. 'Everyone knows your Timothy ain't no angel!'

'Please, ladies and gentlemen! This is neither the time nor the place for personal slurs!' The vicar was on his feet now, looking as if he had a bad smell under his nose. 'Miss Rice has asked for toy sheep, or perhaps we should ask for volunteers to make appropriate costumes. Do we have any takers?'

'No need for that when I have the real thing on my farm!' Oliver Bassett said. 'I can supply as many sheep as you want. Just say the word and I'll have them here on the dot!'

'Sheep?' A female voice squeaked. 'Here in the hall, what I has to scrub down on my hands and knees every

Monday morning? Not blinking likely! And if you think those dirty brutes can follow the kiddies into the church like Mary's little lamb, you can jolly well think again! Isn't that so, vicar?'

Mr Blunt looked sick. 'On the night of our Saviour's birth, the sheep were definitely kept outside,' he said. 'I quote: 'And there were in the same country shepherds abiding in the field, keeping watch over their flocks by night.' *In the field*, mark you. Not indoors.'

'But there were animals in the stable, weren't there, vicar? You know, ox, ass, and sheep.'

'And camels!' someone else shouted. 'Them kings must have come on camels. They couldn't have come all that way from the East on foot and still got there in time to see the Baby.'

'And where are we going to find camels in Llandyfan, you fool?' some one else called.

Maudie could feel a nasty headache coming on. With an apologetic grimace in Joan Blunt's direction, she stood up and made her escape.

'I'm so sorry,' she told her friend the following day. 'I couldn't stand it for another minute. I just felt I had to get away. Why do these village meetings always degenerate into chaos?'

'It was utterly ridiculous, of course,' Mrs Blunt agreed. 'Just the thought of letting cattle and sheep into the parish hall is enough to give me the vapours! And then, of course, Harold tried to explain that there is absolutely nothing in the Gospels about animals around the manger. That didn't go down well at all! There are just too many carols and religious works of art that have led us to believe that there were.'

'I suppose there may have been animals in the stable, though, don't you think? Or would the innkeeper have turned them all out so that Mary could have a nice clean environment to give birth in? Not that they knew much about germs and infections back then. And all those pictures you see of Joseph leading a donkey may have had some basis in truth.

After all, the poor girl was nine months'
pregnant when they travelled to Bethlehem. I doubt she could have managed the
journey on foot.'

'You could be right, Nurse.'

'So what conclusion did the meeting
come to in the end?'

'Some of the men have agreed to erect
a sort of shelter between the church and
the hall, in which there will be a manger
scene — complete with real, live animals.
Harold isn't thrilled, but he's agreed to go
along with it. It's a compromise of sorts.'

11

Maudie dressed for their evening out with a heavy heart. She and Dick were due to go to a Christmas party at the Midvale police station, but she knew that she wouldn't have a moment's peace until they were safely home again. The event was billed as a family do, with police officers and detectives past and present, as well as a number of special constables. These men and women had been invited to bring their spouses along, as well as any children and grandchildren who might be living in the area. And of course, what was a Christmas party without Father Christmas being there to hand out gifts for the kiddies?

That was what was causing Maudie deep concern; for this would not be a professional Father Christmas hired for the occasion, but Dick Bryant, under-cover.

'Why does it have to be you?' she

complained. 'Don't you have anybody with a black belt in judo who could give the villain his comeuppance?'

Dick patted her on the hand. 'Because this is my case, Maudie. Anyway, you don't have to worry. The rest of the team will be nearby, waiting to pounce. We'll have the chap in handcuffs before you can blink twice. Just you wait and see.'

'I hope you're right,' she muttered.

On the face of it, the detective squad had laid their plans well. DI Goodman had taken the editor of the *Chronicle* into his confidence, and a neat little paragraph had been inserted into the coming events page to the effect that a staff party was in the works, complete with a visit from Father Christmas for the kiddies.

'And let's hope the villain reads the *Chronicle*,' Goodman said, 'or our plan may come to nothing.'

'Everyone reads the *Chronicle*,' the editor said with confidence.

'How is this going to work?' Maudie wanted to know. 'You and I are supposed to be going together, but if this mugger is watching to see Father Christmas arrive, it's bound to give the game away when he spots me on my own.'

'You could always dress up as Mrs Christmas.'

'Don't joke about this, Dick Bryant! Can't you see I'm worried?'

'I'll arrive in mufti and get dressed up in the gents'. After I've done my stuff with the kiddies, I'll step outside with a few of the lads, making it look as if we're having a smoke. After a bit, I'll wave them goodbye and walk off down the street. With any luck, the mugger will take the hint and follow.'

'If he's got any sense, he'll suspect a set-up and scarper.'

'We'll have to wait and see, that's all.'

★　★　★

Maudie wasn't willing to trust to luck when it came to her husband's safety, so before the night of the party, she laid plans of her own.

'I don't think we should take Charlie to this knees-up,' she told Dick. 'He's a bit young for that sort of thing, and you're likely to be tied up with your case and not available to run us home if he gets fractious. I've spoken to Joan Blunt and she's delighted to have him at the vicarage for a couple of hours. She'll take Rover as well, so we can go to the party with no qualms.'

'Well, if that's what you'd like, old girl.'

What she would really like would be to stay at home and not go within a mile of the police station, but that would mean letting Dick go without her. No, she had to put her glad rags on, attempt to do something to her face and hair, and go forward into battle.

She did not enjoy the party. The action seemed to consist of police officers talking shop, while their wives, abandoned, stood around in clumps making meaningless conversation. Small children darted about, shrieking, and at one point it looked as if they'd managed to capsize the small fir tree in the corner, until a burly special constable managed to reach out in time to steady it.

At last Dick appeared, resplendent in his traditional robes. After the requisite shouts of *Ho! Ho! Ho!*, he proceeded to hand out small parcels — wrapped in pink for girls and green for boys — while DI Goodman distributed bags of sweets at a brisk pace.

'Green?' Maudie queried, raising her eyebrows at the Inspector's wife who happened to be standing nearby.

'Did you ever try to find blue tissue paper at this time of year?' Mrs Goodman responded. 'It was only by chance that I came across some sheets of pink in a little back-street stationer's. Bentham's has red paper galore, of course, or holly-covered stuff. 'Tis the season, I suppose.'

'And what are you giving the youngsters?'

'Sparkly bangles for the girls, and pea whistles for the boys. Bringing them up to be good little coppers. Whoops! Here we go!'

The boys had discovered their whistles and were making as much noise as possible. Bent over with her fingers in her ears, Maudie missed Dick's farewell remarks, and when she looked in his direction again it was to see that he had gone. Well, she could put her plan into action now without rousing anyone's suspicions. Under cover of the resulting chaos, she slipped out of a side door and found herself standing on a quiet residential street, deserted except for a skulking tomcat.

Dick and his colleagues would be standing about on the front steps by now. At any moment he'd be on the move, although she had no idea of the direction he'd be taking. She moved into the shadow cast by a giant monkey puzzle tree in a nearby front garden.

If Dick came this way, she would watch and wait. If he failed to appear, she would gradually move along the side of the building in the hope of seeing what was happening. She would not, of course, attempt to interfere with a police operation; but if anything went wrong and Dick was under attack, she would rush to his aid and face the consequences later!

Of course she wasn't armed! She wished now that she'd brought some useful tool with her — a good old-fashioned hatpin, say — but she had a good set of lungs to bellow with! If she saw her husband being set upon by thugs, she would stand there and scream her head off until help came. And if DI Goodman didn't like it, that was just too bad. As a nurse, she had seen too many people suffering from a battering, and had no intention of seeing Dick spending a miserable Christmas in hospital with multiple fractures!

She stiffened. Something was happening further down the street. *Yes!* She recognized the sturdy figure of Dick Bryant, made bulkier by the scarlet robes of jolly old Saint Nick. Puzzled, she stood still, observing his slow progress. Why was he coming from that direction? She supposed he must have nipped down some other street so as to give himself maximum exposure to the lurking villain.

Something moved in the shadows. She held her breath. Was this it? Was this the attacker, about to strike? Where were the police hiding? Would help come in time?

The dark shadow sprang forward, one arm raised to strike. Father Christmas plodded on. The attacker struck, and struck again. The red-robed figure fell to the ground and lay still.

'You brute! You beast!' With no thought for her own safety, Maudie charged down the street, her legs going like pistons. By the time she arrived at Dick's side, the attacker had disappeared, but she didn't care.

She knelt down, tearing her new pair of nylons in the process. Pieces of gravel cut into her knees, but she hardly felt the pain.

'Dick! Oh, Dick! Are you all right? Can you hear me? Let me see!' She peeled back the hood of his costume and smothered his forehead with kisses.

'Gerroff, lady! Lemme alone!' That growl of protest certainly hadn't come from Dick Bryant. Scrambling to her feet, Maudie stared down at the victim in horror. She froze again at the sound of running steps, but this time it was all right. The police had arrived in large numbers.

A familiar voice sounded in her ear. Maudie shuddered.

'What in the name of . . . '

'I thought it was you!' she quavered. 'I thought you might be dead!' She turned to her husband, expecting to be taken into his arms and comforted, but he moved away to join his colleagues who were bending over the fallen Father Christmas.

'I'll speak to you later!' he called back over his shoulder, his tone dripping with ice. 'At home. In the meantime, you had better go back to the station and wait for me there. This is no place for amateurs.'

Chagrined, Maudie did as she was told. Hot tears ran down her cheeks, unchecked. She fumbled for a handkerchief, realizing too late that she had come outside without her coat. She had been too concerned about Dick's safety to mind the cold night air, but now it struck her like a blow, and she began to shake. And the December frost was as nothing compared with the chill that lay between her and the man she loved.

12

Another December morning had arrived, bringing with it fine weather but no improvement on the relationship front. Dick had been ominously silent during the drive home the night before, and Maudie hadn't dared to start a conversation. Better to wait until they were safely home, perhaps sitting in front of the fire with cups of cocoa, she thought.

But things hadn't worked out that way. On reaching the vicarage, they had been greeted with a howling Charlie and the vicar's wife, who was clearly distressed by her failure to keep him happy.

'I can't think what's the matter,' she said, her kindly face creased in dismay. 'He's been fed and changed, but nothing seems to pacify him. I do hope he's not coming down with something nasty.'

'He'll be fine once we get him home,' Dick said, taking his son into his arms. 'Thanks for looking after him for us.' He turned to go, with Rover at his heels. Maudie had no choice but to echo his words of thanks and follow him home.

Once there, Charlie had continued to roar. Pacing up and down with the child slung over her shoulder, Maudie hardly noticed when Dick took himself up to bed without saying goodnight.

Apparently having worn himself out the evening before, Charlie slept on past his usual time, which in turn caused his mother to oversleep as well. When she struggled out of bed, she found that Dick had already left for work. The remains of a loaf of bread and a pat of butter had been left out on the kitchen table, showing that he had eaten a scrappy breakfast before leaving the house. There had been no cups of tea brought to Maudie in bed this morning!

Well, let him sulk, if that was what he was doing! What was the matter with the man? He had no need to treat her so meanly! What had she done that was so very wrong, after all? Let him give her the cold shoulder. He would have to come to his senses sooner or later!

She swallowed a sob. This was their very first real quarrel. Did it spell the beginning of the end for them? She sniffed, reaching for her handkerchief. It wasn't like her to go to pieces! This was Midwife Maudie who had brought dozens of babies into the world, sometimes under dreadfully dangerous conditions. She must pull herself together and hope that this bit of fuss would soon blow over; and she would start by making herself a strong pot of tea!

When the doorbell rang she rushed to answer it, hoping against hope that Dick had had second thoughts and had returned to make his peace with her. Highly unlikely, of course, that he'd ring the doorbell when he had his own key!

Joan Blunt stood on the doorstep. 'Hello, Nurse! I hope I haven't come at an inconvenient time.'

Maudie was acutely aware of her unkempt appearance: red-eyed, face unwashed, hair uncombed. 'No, no, of course not. Do come in. I've just made a pot of tea. Would you care to join me?'

'I don't mind if I do! How is young Charlie this morning? I hope he's recovered from his little bout of misery?'

'He's not up yet. Sleeping like a little angel.'

'Good. Good. Now then, I've just popped in to bring you this.' She handed Maudie a gaily wrapped package which, when torn open, revealed a bright yellow rubber duck.

'How kind,' Maudie told her. 'Thank you so much.'

'Oh, it's not from me, Nurse. Mrs Meldrum called in to speak to Harold about something, and she asked me if I'd pass this on to you. You delivered her grandchild back in the spring, of course, and when her daughter heard about Charlie, she wanted to send a little something for his Christmas.'

Maudie felt the treacherous tears flooding to her eyes again, but somehow she was powerless to stop them. Putting her head down on the table, she sobbed aloud. Rover came to her side and looked up at her, moaning softly.

'It's all right, boy,' she told him through

her tears, scratching his ear. 'It's just your silly old missus having a little howl. Nothing to worry about.'

The vicar's wife was no stranger to scenes of woe. It was she, rather than her husband, who often dealt with the angst of his parishioners in times of trouble. She reached out to pat Maudie on the back.

'I don't mean to pry, Nurse, but if there's anything I can do to help . . .'

'It's just me being silly.'

'I think it's a bit more than that, my dear. Do feel free to confide in me. I promise you that whatever you say will be held in complete confidence. It won't go any further. I shan't even say anything to Harold without your permission.' She reached for the teapot and filled each of their cups.

Maudie took a deep breath. 'Dick and I have had a falling-out,' she began. 'Not even a real row, really; but it's the first time it's happened, and I don't know what I should do next.'

'I sensed a bit of tension between you when you came to collect the baby last night. Did something happen at the party?'

'It has to do with those attacks on Father Christmas. They are not making quick progress with the case, and so Dick volunteered to go undercover. The silly fool was supposed to wander around the streets of Midvale in costume, in the hope that the attacker would take the bait and bash him over the head.'

'Oh, dear! Well, I suppose it's all part of his job, isn't it? And no doubt his colleagues would be hiding nearby, ready to capture the chap when he struck.'

'That was the plan, but that didn't mean that Dick couldn't have been seriously hurt in the meantime.'

'Yes, I see. So you spoke out of turn, was that it? Told his boss a few home truths while you were at it?'

'Not a bit of it! All I did was to go outside and keep watch. I just wanted to see what was going on.'

'And if you happened to notice somebody stalking Dick, you meant to rush in and make a citizen's arrest, was that it?'

'Certainly not! I might have screamed for help, but so what? Any onlooker might have done that.'

'So why is your husband so annoyed with you?'

'Because I tried to help, and the attacker got away before they could make an arrest, that's why.'

'You mean that Dick was attacked?'

'I mean that I saw Father Christmas being followed by a shadowy figure. Naturally, I thought that Dick was in danger, but there was no sign of the other officers at all — so when he was knocked down and didn't get up, of course I had to do something!'

'Of course you did. Any wife would have done the same.'

'The trouble is, it wasn't Dick at all. It was some other Father Christmas, and when I tried to comfort him he yelled at me to get lost. His exact words were 'Gerroff, lady', the ungrateful brute.'

Joan Blunt threw back her head and gurgled with laughter. Maudie regarded her crossly.

'I'm sure I don't know what you're

laughing at, Mrs Blunt! I don't find it at all amusing, and I ruined a good pair of nylons in the process!'

'Never mind, dear. I'm sure you'll see the funny side eventually.'

'Dick won't,' Maudie muttered.

'I think you underestimate him, Nurse. Your husband cares for you deeply, and when he's had time to think things through, he'll realize that you only had his best interests at heart.'

'I hope you're right,' Maudie said, reaching for the teapot.

13

When Maudie called in at the village shop, she found Mrs Hatch preoccupied.

'Sorry, Nurse! What was it you wanted again?'

'Eggs, Mrs Hatch. I'm making toad-in-the-hole for our tea, and I need an egg for the Yorkshire pudding.'

'You've left it a bit late for making your Christmas puddings, dear. You should have done them the week after Stir-up Sunday.'

'I did,' Maudie informed her. 'I'm making a batter pudding now, for toad-in-the-hole.'

Mrs Hatch blinked. 'Of course you are, dear. Making your hubby his favourite for his tea, are you? That's the way to keep a man happy, I always say!'

Maudie stared at the postmistress. The woman should know by now that anything made with corned beef was Dick's favourite; enough cans of the stuff had been purchased here in the past two years to sink a battleship.

'Are you all right, Mrs Hatch? Is there something worrying you? Only, you seem a bit distraught this morning.'

'Camels!'

'I beg your pardon?'

'It's this business of the Christmas pageant. The men are building a sort of manger scene between the church and the parish hall in which to put real, live animals.'

'Yes, I did hear that.'

'So Oliver Bassett is bringing a few sheep along, and old Will Price is lending us his donkey.'

'And?'

'And those fool men have decided we need a camel or two; preferably three.'

'I thought the vicar put paid to that? There's nothing about camels in the Bible, is there? At least,' she amended, 'not in the Nativity story.'

'Yes, but those three wise men couldn't have got there so fast unless they had camels. Stands to reason! If they'd had to walk all that way from the East, they wouldn't have seen the baby Jesus before Joseph took him away to Egypt, to escape from that wicked King Herod.'

'I suppose you're right, Mrs Hatch.'

'Yes, well, those men say they have enough to do, building the stable and that, so it's up to the Mothers' Union to provide the camels.'

'Perhaps one would be enough, just to give a *suggestion* of camels,' Maudie said. 'Have you thought of hiring a pantomime horse and putting a hump on it? You could put two of the men inside it; and serve them right, too!' She chuckled to herself.

'It's all very well for you to laugh, Nurse Bryant! This is the panto season, isn't it? All the costumes and bits of scenery are all spoken for until after the New Year.'

'That's it, Mrs Hatch! All we need is a big screen, or a tarpaulin or something, to use as a backdrop to the manger scene. Somebody can paint a couple of camels on it, and there we are, problem solved!'

'Well, I suppose that might do it. How are you fixed for lending a hand, Nurse?'

Maudie backtracked in a hurry. 'I'm afraid I'm not the least bit artistic, Mrs Hatch! Besides, I've got the baby, and he's being a bit of a handful at the moment. I simply don't have a minute to spare.'

They both looked at Charlie, whose innocent blue eyes belied his mother's words.

'Looks to me like butter wouldn't melt in his mouth,' Mrs Hatch said. 'What about your hubby, then? I know he's a dab hand with a paintbrush because he's been making those toy building bricks for the little boy.'

Serve him right if I dropped him in it, Maudie thought, but she was in enough trouble already. It was best to be on the safe side. 'Dick is quite busy at present, 'she murmured. 'It's this business of the attacks on Father Christmas, you know. Dick's boss is keeping them all hard at it. He wants the case sewn up before Christmas, you see.'

'Well, he'd have to, wouldn't he? You won't find many Father Christmases roaming the streets come the New Year.'

She handed Maudie half a dozen eggs, nestled in straw in a cardboard box that had once held envelopes. Stowing them away in the pram, well out of reach of Charlie's tiny fists, Maudie made her escape. Camels, indeed! What next?

★ ★ ★

The sound of hammering reached Maudie's ears that afternoon, and needless to say, the other members of her household heard it too. Charlie refused to settle to his customary nap, and Rover, too, was perturbed by the unusual noise. He gave the alarm at frequent intervals, setting Charlie off again. At last, Maudie had had enough. Packing the baby into his pram and attaching the dog's lead to the handle, she set off in the direction of the church. She found the vicar and his wife gloomily surveying the mess of planks and ladders beside the gravel path leading from the parish hall to the ancient house of worship.

'I still say we should use the lych gate, Vicar! T'would save us a might of time and trouble. We can put the crib in there, for the stable, like; and then all we has to do is put up a fence to pen the livestock in.'

Looking on, Maudie thought it sounded like a great idea. It was easy to imagine the old lych gate, with its peaked roof, as a stable in Bethlehem; and the chap was quite right, it would save a lot of time and labour. Traditionally, a lych gate played a part in funerals, when the pallbearers could rest the coffin there for a few moments before carrying it into the church. But even if somebody died, there would not be a funeral on Christmas Eve, so where was the problem?

'Absolutely not!' Harold Blunt roared. His wife plucked at his sleeve nervously, but he shook her off. 'People come through that gate on their way to church! How are they supposed to manage if the thing is blocked off by a manger scene?'

'Go round the outside, Vicar.'

'And what if it rains and the graveyard is a sea of mud? Oh, that will go down well, I'm sure! People getting their best shoes clogged with mud, to say nothing of the mess the church cleaners will have to deal with later on. I've given my permission — reluctantly — for this outdoor extravaganza, on the understanding that it will involve a modest and temporary structure, but that's as far as it goes. Do I make myself clear?'

Without giving the man time to reply, the vicar turned and marched towards the vicarage.

'So much for the Christmas spirit,' Joan Blunt sighed, coming to stand beside Maudie. 'I don't know why we couldn't have left everything as usual, with the pageant at the school where it belongs, and the services in the church. It's a dreadful thing to say, but one way and another I'll be glad when Christmas 1951 is behind us!'

'I blame it on the war,' Maudie said.

'How do you make that out, then?'

'Well, I know the war's been over for six years, but the country is only just beginning to get back to normal. We've still had rationing until recently, and so many things have been in short supply.

People are desperate to forget all that now and return to a time of plenty. Unfortunately, a sense of greed has crept in as well.'

'I know what you mean. If sweets come off the ration next year, as the politicians are promising us, I dread to think what will happen then! I expect the shops will be mobbed by kiddies trying to find something to spend their pocket money on. It won't surprise me if some people who can afford it will stock up on pounds and pounds of the stuff, leaving nothing for others.'

'I must say, I'll be first in line when that time comes,' Maudie told her, grinning. 'I haven't tasted Turkish Delight since 1940.'

'I'm sure your husband will find some for you,' Joan Blunt said — which was rather tactless of her, Maudie thought, considering that she knew about the current rift between the Bryants.

'I'd better be getting back, Mrs Blunt. Charlie's nappies are still on the line, and it looks as if it's coming on to rain.' Maudie tried to summon up a smile, but it failed to reach her eyes. Mrs Blunt stood staring after her friend, biting her lip. Should she try to intervene, she wondered, or was it best to mind her own business? So often, it was hard to know.

14

When Maudie rounded the corner onto her own street the first thing she noticed was a slight figure leaning over her gate. Well, *draped* was a better word, she told herself; for to all appearances it was somebody in distress, most likely needing the services of a nurse or midwife. She quickened her pace, but not before Rover had given a sharp warning bark, straining at the leash that tethered him to the pram, causing it to wobble.

'Steady on, old boy!' she cautioned, but it was too late. The pram leapt forward with Maudie in tow, just as the figure straightened, stumbling sideways in an effort to avoid a collision. It was the infants teacher, Gwyneth Probert.

'Sorry!' Maudie puffed. 'I'm afraid my dog is a bit overexcited. Did you want to see me about something?'

'If it's not too much trouble . . . ' The girl faltered.

'Right, then. Let's go inside, shall we? We'll have a cup of tea, and you can tell me all about it.'

Once indoors, Maudie put the kettle on before making the excuse that Charlie needed changing and she wanted to put him down for a nap. 'I shan't be long, Miss Probert. Keep an eye on that kettle if you will, and heat the pot when the water boils.'

Playing for time, she took the baby upstairs. Apart from red-rimmed eyes, the girl didn't look ill. Surely to goodness she hadn't come here to find out if she was pregnant? The well-known expression 'in trouble' would be particularly appropriate here if this were the case. The Llandyfan school was a Church of England institution, and when the girl's secret came out it would mean instant dismissal. What would she do then? Presumably she would return to the Welsh valley from which she had come, but what sort of reception would she get there?

Maudie had seen the film *How Green Was My Valley* — had, in fact, sat through it twice, gripped by the tension of social life in a Welsh mining community under the sway of the chapel. She could imagine poor Gwyneth being forced to appear before the congregation, her shame laid bare for all to see, while fire and brimstone gushed from the mouth of some black-clad minister.

'Well, I suppose I'd better go and deal with it,' she told Charlie, who gurgled in response.

When the girl was settled at the kitchen table with a strong cup of tea in front of her, Maudie took a deep breath and began. 'Now, then, what was it you wanted to see me about, Miss Probert?'

'Oh, I'm in such trouble, Mrs Bryant!'

'Oh, yes?'

'It's because I'm Chapel, see?'

Maudie scratched her forehead. It was just as she'd thought. Perhaps if she sat quietly without saying much, the whole sorry tale would come out. She nodded wisely.

'One of the mothers came and spoke to me after school. Not very kind, she was. I was on playground duty — making sure that the children leave the premises safely, you know — and she had come to collect her little girl. She came right up to me and said she wanted to speak to me for my own good. Then she told me that I must go away quietly, and not bring sorrow to honest people who had lived here in this place before I was even born.'

'I say, that's a bit thick! How did she even know about you, anyway?'

Miss Probert frowned. 'Why, it was announced at the meeting, wasn't it? You were there, Mrs Bryant; you must have heard.'

'Announced?' Now it was Maudie's turn to look puzzled.

'That I'm to perform a solo or two at the carol service in the church.'

'Oh, that.'

'Yes, of course. What did you think I meant?'

'Never mind. Do go on.'

'The mother who spoke to me is Gladys Brown's niece, you see. She said her aunt has faithfully sung in the choir for donkey's years, and it isn't fair that she should be crowded out by a chit of a girl who isn't even Church of England.

Her poor Auntie Glad feels let down and unappreciated, and she's sure that everyone pities her for being cast aside like an old jumper that's too far gone even to send to the Salvation Army.'

'Ah, I see.'

'And then she went on to tell me how some of the parents feel I should never have been hired to teach in a church school, what with me being a nonconformist.'

'I'm sure this is just a storm in a tea cup, Miss Probert. Why don't you have a word with the vicar? I'm sure this can all be straightened out in no time.'

'Oh, I couldn't do that! Can't you say something, Mrs Bryant? He might listen to you.'

'Well, if you really want me to, I suppose I could,' said Maudie. 'But I can't do it now when I've just put the baby down. I'll pop over in the morning. Just as a matter of interest, why did you come to see me about this? Of course I'm pleased to be of assistance, but it's not exactly a nursing matter, is it?'

The girl blushed. 'Oh, I didn't really. After she left — the niece, that is — I was so upset, I just had to go for a walk to try to calm myself down. I'd just reached your gate when the whole business got the better of me, and I leaned on it for support. There was nobody about, so I thought it didn't matter if I let myself go for a few minutes.'

'Oh, well, no harm done.' Maudie waved the teapot in Miss Probert's direction but the girl stood up, shaking her head.

'You've been very kind, Mrs Bryant, but I must be going. Thank you for listening to my silly little troubles.'

'Not at all,' Maudie said, smiling.

When the young teacher had gone, Maudie busied herself with her preparations for the evening meal. What a mix-up! She could well understand why Gladys Brown might be hurt and annoyed. And who was at fault here? The headmistress, Miss Rice, seemed to have acted without thinking; although of course it was entirely up to her to rule on matters concerning the school. The unfortunate part of the muddle was that people appeared to be taking sides, and poor Gwyneth Probert, an innocent bystander, was bearing the brunt of it.

Maudie felt that she wouldn't be in the vicar's shoes for any amount of money. He would need the wisdom of Solomon to sort this one out unless his congregation was to be divided for years to come. Sadly, the Reverend Harold Blunt, committed Christian though he was, had been known to lose his temper occasionally. He was one of those mild-mannered people who went along for years without ever having a fit of pique — but then, if they felt strongly enough about an issue, suddenly erupted in an explosion to rival Vesuvius.

So much for the season of peace and goodwill if the vicar mounted his pulpit to unleash some good old home truths on his unsuspecting flock! Maudie made up her mind to speak to Joan Blunt first. She might be able to dish up the unpalatable facts for her husband in a way that would avert a potential crisis. She would pop over and have a word later that evening, if Dick was at home to keep an ear open for Charlie.

* ★ *

Unbeknownst to Maudie, it was already too late to prevent the former soloist's niece from making further trouble.

'I'm afraid that Clara Bowman has already been here, full of righteous indignation,' Joan Blunt said. 'Fortunately Harold wasn't home at the time, although I know that the evil hour has only been postponed. Heaven knows how many people the woman has already talked to.'

'It's worse than that, I'm afraid. The woman buttonholed Miss Probert in the school playground, and more or less told her she'd better give up the idea of singing at Christmas, or else.'

'Or else what, I wonder?'

'I think that she'd like to see the poor girl drummed out of the school because she isn't a member of our church.'

Mrs Blunt groaned. 'Isn't that just what we need on top of everything else! I'm afraid Harold will have to be told about this, but he won't like it. He won't like it at all.'

15

What might be described as an armed truce prevailed in the Bryant household. Dick came home from work in good time for tea, making no reference to the debacle of the Christmas party. When she heard his key in the lock, Maudie tensed, not knowing what to expect, but it appeared that the subject wasn't up for debate; at least, not yet. He patted his son on the head with a few words of endearment; Rover received similar treatment. There was no loving pat for Maudie. Well, two could play at that game!

'Tea will be ready shortly,' she said, keeping her tone light and pleasant. She wouldn't ask him how his day had been: it was caring about his welfare that had got her into trouble, so she would just say nothing.

She dished up a meal that was tasty enough: rissoles made from leftover roast beef, mashed potatoes and diced carrots. None of it included any of his favourite things; in fact, he disliked carrots, and usually left a few bits on his plate. But if she had prepared a special meal for him, it would look as if she was making some sort of apology, which was certainly not the case.

'I'm off down the pub,' he told her, when he had eaten the last of the tapioca pudding and raspberry jam.

'Right. See you later,' Maudie responded.

This was a new departure! Dick was not a heavy drinker, and he seldom went to the Royal Oak. He was not one of those men who used their local pub as a sort of social club where they could get together with their mates. He and Maudie occasionally went there together for a pub lunch, although that hadn't happened since the birth of young Charlie.

She didn't hear the car start up, so he must have decided to walk. Perhaps he needed to clear his head. Miserably, she cleared the last of the crockery from the table and went to wash up.

It was after closing time when he returned. She noted that he didn't seem the worse for wear, so he must not have been drowning his sorrows. Was that a good sign?

'I'm off up, then,' he told her, heading for the stairs. She nodded, deliberately finishing the row she was knitting so as not to appear too eager. When at last she joined him, she saw that he was lying as close to the edge of the bed as he could manage without actually falling out.

'Ungrateful brute!' she muttered. There was no reply from her husband.

* * *

Weather-wise, at least, the next morning was one to lift the spirits. There had been a hoar frost overnight and now a watery sun was struggling to show itself, making the trees look as if they had been sprinkled with silvery tinsel. Dick had taken himself off to work, as morose as he'd been the previous evening, and Maudie was determined not to let their continued rift get her down. Why waste such a beautiful day? She had been meaning to call on Cora Beasley, and this was as good a time as any.

The wealthy Mrs Beasley was Llandyfan's equivalent to the lady of the manor. Her elegant Georgian house, situated two miles outside the village, stood in several acres of land, and the estate also owned several other properties, worked by tenant farmers. Something akin to an old-fashioned feudal system remained in the area, with the elderly widow being expected to hold various offices within the parish. Among other things, she was president of the Mothers' Union, and a governor of the village school.

Mrs. Beasley and Maudie had been on good terms ever since they had been held hostage by a murderer some years earlier, only escaping with their lives when a distraught father-to-be had fortuitously arrived on the scene to summon Maudie to his wife's bedside.

Mrs Beasley greeted Maudie with pleasure. 'Do come in, Nurse! I'm just about to have morning coffee. Will you join me?'

'Yes, please!' Maudie knew Mrs Beasley's coffee of old. Made with boiled milk and a good squirt of rum, it was just the thing for a frosty morning. 'What about Rover?' she asked. 'Should I leave him outside?'

'No, no. Do bring him in. Poor little chap; we don't want him getting frostbitten paws, do we? And you can bring the pram through to the sitting room. I'm sure the wheels aren't muddy on a day like this. And I'm glad you've called, Nurse, because you've saved me a trip. I have a little something for your son's Christmas stocking.' She produced a gaily wrapped package that jingled as she passed it to Maudie. Charlie's eyes opened wide at the sound.

'Ah, yes, I thought that might amuse him! Don't let him have it now, though, Nurse. Save it for Christmas Day.'

When Mrs Beasley's maid had placed a steaming cup in front of Maudie, it was time to get down to business. 'I have a problem, Mrs Beasley. At least, it's not really anything to do with me, but I'm concerned about the wellbeing of a young girl I know of.'

'I suppose you mean Miss Probert at the school? We've got ourselves into a bit of a muddle there, I'm afraid.'

'Ah,' Maudie said. She had come to discuss the problem of Lily Rose Croome, but that could wait. 'I happened to come across Miss Probert who was in some distress. Not that I was trying to interfere in a school matter,' she added hastily. 'She was leaning on my garden gate having a little weep, so naturally I had to take her inside and see what I could do to help.'

'Of course. And did you manage to get to the bottom of what was troubling her?'

'It's rather nasty, I'm afraid. Mrs Brown's niece called on her in the school playground and gave her a proper telling-off. In fact, she suggested that the poor child has no business teaching in a church school when she's a nonconformist.'

Mrs Beasley sighed. 'We were lucky to get Miss Probert to take on the job. What people like Gladys Brown's niece don't seem to realize is that we can't offer the sort of salary that would attract too many people. Little Miss Probert is well-qualified, and if she hadn't accepted the post we'd have been in a real fix this past term.'

'It is a pity about Gladys Brown, though. She must feel so hurt being cast aside after forty years of faithful service.'

'It didn't happen quite like that,' Cora Beasley said. 'As you may know, Nurse, the school performance is to take place in the parish hall, after which everybody will go into the church for the carol service. When Miss Rice announced that the infants teacher would perform a solo, I believe she meant that to occur as part of the school's contribution. In the hall, do you see? Or even perhaps when they were marching in a crocodile over to the carol service. Someone jumped to the wrong conclusion, that was all.'

'That seems odd to me.'

Mrs Beasley grimaced. 'I'm afraid that poor Mrs Brown's voice isn't what it used to be. She sometimes has trouble reaching the high notes, and her performance is marred by throat-clearing and the occasional cough. The difficulty is that nobody likes to tell her it's time to step down. If only she'd announce her retirement, we could present her with a nice gift in recognition of her years of service, and honour would be satisfied. As it is, we are left with a situation like this, where some of the faithful are saying its time for her to go, while others remain staunchly on her side. This school concert has brought the situation to a head in a way we hadn't foreseen.'

'It seems to me that there shouldn't be a problem in the short term,' Maudie said. 'The vicar can announce that it's all been a misunderstanding. Miss Probert sings in the parish hall; Gladys Brown performs in the church as always.'

'And will Miss Probert be content with that, do you think?'

'I imagine she'll do anything to avoid the wrath of Gladys Brown's supporters. However, that isn't why I've come, Mrs Beasley. I recently met a Mrs Croome, who had come over from Brookfield in the hope of having a word with you. Did she actually turn up?'

'Croome? No, I'm sure she didn't. I do employ a man of that name at Brookfield, however. Perhaps this was his wife?'

'Yes, that's what she said.'

'But what did she want with me? I hope she hadn't come to plead with me to increase his wages! I leave all that sort of thing to my estate manager.'

'It seems they have a teenage daughter who has got herself into trouble. It's the old, old story. The young man in the picture doesn't want to know, and he's done a bunk. Meanwhile, the girl's father has shown her the door, and his wife is frantic.'

'As well she might be. And I suppose Croome has forbidden the woman to have any contact with their daughter?'

'It's worse than that. She has no idea where the girl could be, and by now she must be nearing her time. The family belong to a strict religious sect at Brookfield, and my guess is that the girl has run away from their influence as much as anything else. I gather that Mrs Croome meant to ask you to put pressure on her husband — force him to allow the

136

girl to be traced, on pain of getting the sack — but she thought better of it at the last moment.'

'Couldn't DS Bryant . . . ?'

'He did speak to one or two of the sect's members, but they all seem to be upright citizens and he could find no excuse for putting pressure on them, especially as this Lily Rose hasn't been officially reported as a missing person.'

'So now you've turned to me. What exactly do you expect me to do, Nurse?'

Maudie shrugged. 'I have no idea why I've come, really. I only know that I can't bear to think of that poor child giving birth all alone in a squat somewhere, or even in the out-of-doors. So much could go wrong, Mrs Beasley. It doesn't bear thinking about.'

Cora Beasley stared at her visitor for a long moment. Then she stood up, straightening the skirt of her purple woollen jumper suit. 'Well, Nurse, it's plain to see that something must be done, and you and I must act in this matter. And there is no time like the present!'

16

Maudie sat squashed in the back seat of Cora Beasley's shiny Lanchester, holding Charlie on her lap. The rest of the seat was taken up with Mrs Beasley's considerable bulk. Rover, panting happily, occupied the passenger seat in the front.

When this expedition was first suggested, Maudie had hesitated. She wasn't sure how proficient Mrs Beasley's driving was, and she had Charlie's safety to think of; but when she learned that the lady's chauffeur would be at the wheel, she quickly agreed to go along.

Mrs Beasley explained that the few acres of land she owned outside Brookfield had been planted with evergreen trees shortly after the war. 'It was no good for anything else. The local council had taken over part of it to put up prefabs when new housing was so badly needed, and what was left wasn't enough even for a decent smallholding. So we put in a lot of pines and spruces.'

'But you employ men there?' Maudie queried. 'Don't the trees more or less look after themselves, then?'

'Oh, no, Nurse. A plantation has to be properly managed, you know. Trees have to be pruned, and they need to be sprayed when they're attacked by pests, or they'll soon die off. And one must weed out the natural trees and shrubs that tend to choke out the trees one hopes to preserve. Evergreens are not much more than a foot high when they are first put into the ground, you know. They need careful nurturing in order to survive.'

On arrival at the plantation, they were met by a workman who touched his cap to Mrs Beasley while casting a curious glance at Maudie, bringing up the rear with a baby on her hip. Freed from the confines of the car, Rover bounced around, yelping joyously.

'I wish to speak with Croome,' Mrs Beasley told him. 'Is he here?'

'Yes, madam. He's in the hut, making our tea. Shall I tell him he's wanted?'

Ivan Croome, when he appeared, was

not at all what Maudie had imagined. She had imagined a tall, burly man, possibly with mutton-chop whiskers, the epitome of a stern Victorian father. Croome, however, was a little bandy-legged man, rather stooped. If she had met him anywhere else, she might have taken him for a retired jockey; although given his stern religious principles, that would hardly have been likely.

Mrs Beasley wasted no time. 'We have come about your daughter,' she said.

'Ain't got no daughter, missus.'

'Come now, man, I happen to know that you are the parent of a seventeen-year-old girl who is sadly in need of your help.'

'She gave up her right to that when she went astray,' he said, twisting his greasy cap in his gnarled hands. He appeared to have noticed Maudie for the first time. 'And if that there's the fruit of her sin, you can just take it back where it came from. We don't want the likes of that here!'

Maudie stared back at him indignantly. 'I'll have you know, I'm a respectable

140

married woman, and this is my son! But if this had been your grandchild, I hope you would have taken a different attitude to this!'

'Conceived in sin! We want no part of it here!'

'An innocent child, Mr Croome, due to be born at Christmastime. Have you no compassion at all?'

There was no reply to this. The two women exchanged glances.

'I must insist that you allow your wife to attempt to find Lily Rose, Mr Croome; and, if she succeeds, to bring her back under your roof where she belongs. I quite understand that you may not wish the girl to keep the child; but it can be adopted, you know, and I can assist with that. Now, what do you say?'

'I say it isn't none of your business, and I'll thank you to keep your nose out of it!'

Maudie winced, but she was watching the president of the Mothers' Union in action. Mrs Beasley had managed to quell many a near-riot in the ranks, and she wasn't about to back down now.

'Mr Croome, I'm afraid that if you

refuse to cooperate I shall be forced to terminate your employment here.'

'You ain't got no right to make a man go against his principles, missus!'

'Then I hope your principles will put food in your stomach and keep a roof over your head this winter, man.'

'The Lord will provide,' he said, turning away.

'Silly old fool!' Cora Beasley muttered when Croome had disappeared inside the wooden hut. 'Who does he think he is, an early Christian martyr?'

'At least you tried,' Maude murmured.

'Oh, I'm not finished yet, Nurse! We'll go and see the girl's mother. Perhaps we'll get somewhere with her.'

* ★ ★

Rover, meanwhile, was having the time of his life: nosing his way from one tree to the next, following scents that were obviously irresistible to him. A man clad in dirty dungarees was leaning on a shovel nearby, oblivious to the presence of the two women.

There's a chap who needs a good shaking up, Maudie thought. Didn't he care that his employer was on the scene? Or perhaps he didn't realize who Cora Beasley was.

Rover approached the man, sniffing. Something about the man's trousers seemed particularly attractive to the dog, who clamped his teeth on the fabric and began to tug.

The man lashed out with his foot, sending the dog sprawling. 'Gerroff, you silly beggar!' he bawled. 'Gerroff!'

Maudie froze. She knew that tone of voice! Unless she was very much mistaken, this was the man dressed as Father Christmas whom she had rushed in to save, believing him to be Dick.

★ ★ ★

They found Mrs Croome in the end house in a row of terraced dwellings that Cora Beasley identified as a relic of the Victorian era, when such accommodation was provided for farm labourers. The woman's hand flew to her mouth when she saw who her visitors were, but she managed to pull herself together, and quickly invited them inside.

The house was clean, but sparsely furnished. Maudie realized with a pang of dismay that Ivan Croome's forthcoming unemployment would be the cause of utter privation. No doubt he was paid an adequate wage for the work he did, but by the look of things, very little of that money went on luxuries here. Probably he donated a hefty portion to the church they belonged to.

'We've come about your daughter,' Cora Beasley began. Mrs Croome's face lit up with hope.

'You know where she is?'

'Not yet, I'm afraid, but we mean to find out. Unfortunately your husband has refused to cooperate, even in the face of possibly losing his job.'

Mrs Croome sank down on a chair, white-faced. 'Well, I can't say I'm surprised, madam. I knew that might happen when I decided to contact you, so I've only myself to blame. Still, I had to try, didn't I?'

'Of course you did. And of course this isn't your fault. Your husband is a stubborn man who needs a good talking-to. In the meantime, we shall have to proceed without him. Have you any idea where your daughter might have turned for help?'

'Oh, no; I couldn't go behind Ivan's back, madam! That wouldn't be right.'

'Nonsense, woman! Do you want the girl found or not? Just tell me what you know, and leave the wretched man to me!'

Maudie gazed at Mrs Beasley in admiration. This was the spirit that had won the war for Britain!

Timidly, Mrs Croome suggested a number of schoolfriends who might know where Lily Rose was now. 'But I'm afraid she may have gone up to London,' she finished.

'London!' Maudie said. 'Why on earth would she want to go there?'

'Because that's where he's gone; the father of her child. I mean, he gave her a lot of silly talk about wanting to make it as a rock star, and London was where it's happening, whatever that means.'

'But I thought you told me the chap doesn't want to know, and has no intention of standing by her.'

Mrs Croome shrugged. 'That don't stop her hoping, though, do it?'

★   ★   ★

'That woman is a bit of a weak Winnie,' Mrs Beasley observed when they were trooping back to her car, with Rover trotting in their wake. 'It beats me why some women find themselves utterly in thrall to some man, unable to lift a finger to help themselves. Why, if she'd stood up to that husband of hers, the girl would never have gone missing in the first place. When he threatened to throw the child out, his wife should have told him 'If she goes, I go too', and that would have given him something to think about!'

'Hmm,' Maudie said. 'In this case, it probably has something to do with that sect they belong to. Wives are supposed to be handmaidens or something.'

'Phooey! I'd give them handmaidens!'

Hiding a grin, Maudie decided it was

just as well for the men of Brookfield that Mrs Beasley was a pillar of the Church of England! Not that any of this brought them any closer to tracing the pregnant Lily Rose.

★ ★ ★

Having retrieved the pram from the Beasley home and installed her son in it, Maudie set off for home, singing softly as she marched along. '*Good King Wenceslas looked out . . .*'

She stopped suddenly, remembering the uncouth fellow they'd come across at the tree farm. The more she thought about it, the surer she became that this was the chap she'd mistaken for Dick on the night of the Christmas party.

But what did this mean, if anything? She wished she knew what the police had found out when they'd interviewed the stricken Father Christmas. But Dick was tight-lipped about the whole affair; and, in fact, had barely spoken to her since then. She could imagine the reception she'd get if she tried to probe into it now!

On the other hand, she hadn't liked the chap at all. He seemed like a criminal type to her, if there was such a thing. What if he somehow held the key to the mystery of the attacks on Father Christmas? Wasn't it her duty to share with the police any knowledge she might have?

She toyed with the idea of telephoning the Midvale police station and giving a hint to that snooty policewoman who manned the phones there. But she had called there in the past, wanting to speak to Dick, and the woman might recognize her voice.

The only thing to do was to wait until Dick came home and simply blurt out what she knew, risking a snub. Honour would be satisfied — but then what? If he refused to tell her what had happened after the attack, she would feel like hitting him!

Conflicting thoughts went through Maudie's mind. *Drat you, Dick Bryant! Why do you have to behave like a man? Are you a woman or a mouse, Maudie Bryant?* She absolutely refused to remain under his thumb, like that poor specimen of womanhood at Brookfield! She had solved mysteries before, and she could see no reason to change her ways now.

17

Dick Bryant studied his notes for what seemed like the fiftieth time. The cup of tea at his elbow had gone cold, and the Mars Bar in his desk drawer was still in its wrapper. This Father Christmas business was one of the most annoying and puzzling cases he'd ever had to deal with.

It didn't help that the thing was intruding on his home life. He thought he'd never forget DI Goodman's reaction to the debacle of the Christmas party operation.

'Can you not control your wife, Bryant?' That was his chief's only response but the look of disgust on the older man's face said it all. The other men on the team were less reticent. Dick had to endure a lot of remarks about Sherlock Holmes and Doctor Watson that left him in no doubt as to which of the pair he was!

There was nothing he could do but live

it down, and that was easier said than done. Maudie simply had to learn that she must not get involved in police investigations. Until he could convince her of that, his job was at stake. His boss was quite right. Bringing family members into police cases wasn't right, it wasn't professional — and, most of all, it wasn't safe. All right, so Maudie had got herself tangled up in murder and mayhem in the past, but that was precisely where that sort of thing must stay. She was a mother now, and she had responsibilities.

'Get on with your work, Bryant!' he admonished himself. As Goodman kept reminding him, they had only a few more days in which to tidy up this case. Soon the Father Christmas costumes would be packed away for another year, and they might never know what had been behind the attacks on the jolly old man. Other crimes would continue to be perpetrated, including more muggings, but there would be nothing to connect them with the current spate of attacks.

Dick glanced at the statistics he had already compiled. They had identified six different Father Christmases working in the area. As far as they knew, the first to be struck down had been ex-Sergeant John Fry, working in Bentham's department store to supplement his police pension. The most likely explanation was that it was an act of revenge on the part of someone Fry had been instrumental in getting sent to prison. Or perhaps it was the father or son of such a person. DI Goodman was still looking into that. Had any old lags been released from confinement recently? Had anyone died in prison, leaving grieving and vengeful relatives on the outside?

Although that branch of the investigation was still ongoing, the later attack on Alf Morton put a different complexion on the whole affair. Goodman had pointed out: 'This chap had replaced Fry at Bentham's, but possibly the attacker hadn't been aware of that? When the first attempt to kill or maim the former sergeant had failed, perhaps the killer had moved in for another go.'

'It's a possibility, sir,' Dick agreed. 'However, there is the business of the thefts at the post office where Morton works. Perhaps he's part of a larger operation, but decided to skim some extra cash off the top to line his own pockets. His partners in crime decided he had to be taught a lesson, so that's how it went down.'

'True enough, but unless we can get him to talk we may never get to the bottom of that.'

Now, reviewing all this in his mind, Dick sighed. It might well be that the two cases weren't connected at all. At least, that was what he had thought until the night of the Christmas party when yet another Father Christmas had been struck down. Surely that was just too much of a coincidence!

It was too bad that the trap they had laid had failed. It had been the chief's idea that one of his men should masquerade as Father Christmas, walking the district until the attacker took the bait. Other officers would linger nearby, ready to pounce. Goodman had asked for volunteers. Dick's hand had shot up at once.

Now he felt like a fool. He was a middle-aged man, married, with a son. What on earth had possessed him to leap into the fray like a character in *The Boy's Own Paper*? Good police work wasn't about glory and high adventure. It was made up of steady slog and the careful examination of evidence.

'So here's what we do,' Goodman had told his men on the morning before the party. 'We go out on the main steps and hang about, having a smoke. That gives plenty of time for you to get noticed, Bryant. When I give the word, you'll set off down the street while we take up our positions as previously decided. Let's hope it draws the chap out.'

But of course their plan had failed. Over and over again, Dick had replayed the scene in his mind. Somewhere within earshot a woman had started to scream. Whistles blowing, the police team rushed to the rescue with Dick, partly impeded by his crimson robes, bringing up the rear. What he saw when he rounded the corner made his blood run cold.

Stretched across the prone body of his

alter ego was a woman in a light blue coat. He knew that coat, and he knew the wearer. She was moaning now. 'Dick! Oh, Dick!'

She was alive, and seemingly unhurt. Relief, followed by anger, flooded over him. 'I'll speak to you later!'

Occasionally, a distraught woman would come to the police station to report a missing child, perhaps one who had wandered off towards a busy road or a flooded river. Often when the youngster was safely restored to its tearful parent the mother would turn on it in anger, administering a hearty slap to the tot's legs. He had never understood that in the past, but he knew now why that was.

The new Father Christmas had been helped to his feet, dusted off, and taken into the police station for questioning.

'I don't want none of this, neither,' the man protested, after turning down an offer to be driven to Casualty to see a doctor. 'I ain't done nothing wrong.'

'You are not being accused of anything,' DI Goodman told him. 'We'd just like to ask you a few questions, that's all.'

Grumbling, the man allowed himself to be assisted into the station. To Dick's chagrin, he wasn't allowed to sit in on this interview, on the grounds that his presence there would be one Father Christmas too many. 'You get off home,' he was told. 'Mustn't keep the missus out too late, not after what she's just been through, ha ha!'

So Dick had to wait until the next day, when he read the official transcript of the interview, which didn't amount to much in any case. The chap was Samuel Bracken, 59, agricultural labourer, of 32 Riverside Cottages, Brookfield. How was it that he'd been in Midvale to get himself knocked over the head?

'I was hired to put on this clobber and go to a staff party at Barclays Bank, wasn't I?' he explained. 'Anything for a few extra bob, but it wasn't worth it in the end. The party wasn't much of a knees-up. Not even a decent drink to wet a fellow's whistle. All these stuffed shirts standing around drinking sherry. Then I gets clobbered over the head walking back to the bus stop; and the next thing I knows, some fool woman is hugging me and calling me her darling Mick.'

Reading this, Dick blushed. He could just imagine the guffaws that had greeted that remark. The fellow concluded by saying that he didn't get a look at his assailant, had no idea who it could have been, and could think of no reason why he should have been targeted, unless robbery was the motive.

'It won't do any harm to look into this Bracken's background,' Goodman suggested later. 'See if he's got any priors. And while you're at it, have a look at the remaining three Father Christmases. You never know what you might find.'

★ ★ ★

Dick looked up from his notes to find a policewoman approaching his desk.

'The boss wants to see you,' she muttered.

'Sir!'

'Eh?'

''The boss wants to see you, *sir*'!'

'Oh, sorry, *sir*.'

Did he detect a touch of insolence there? Maybe it was his imagination that he had lost face with his colleagues — or perhaps it was only that they looked at him sideways for being so ready to volunteer for special duties.

DI Goodman, however, showed no sign of displeasure when Dick entered his office.

'Ah, there you are, Bryant. How's the nipper? Too young to look forward to Christmas as yet, of course. You have all that to come. Now then, what have you found out about our jolly Saint Nicks?'

'Very little, sir. A couple of drunk and disorderlies against Bracken: appearances in the magistrates' court, and let off with fines. The other three men seem clean; just retired chaps glad to earn a few extra bob at this time of year.'

'Never mind, Bryant; just keep at it. Something may turn up yet, although I'm still inclined towards my original theory — that the intended target was a grudge attack against Fry, and the rest of it just coincidence, more or less. The other chaps could have been got at for any reason at all, from an unpaid debt to a common-or-garden robbery.'

'Yes, sir.' Dick didn't altogether agree with his boss, but there was no point in telling him that, or at least, not at this stage. If only he could discuss this with Maudie! He missed their former easy conversations, but he mustn't give in now. He wouldn't dream of trying to interfere when she was delivering some woman's baby, and she should afford him the same professional courtesy.

18

Outside the village shop, Maudie put the brake on the pram and smiled down at her son. 'You be a good boy while Mummy does her shopping,' she told him. He rewarded her with a beaming smile. Quite often there were one or two other prams parked nearby and the babies would gurgle to each other, but this morning there was nobody else in sight.

She removed Rover's leash from the pram handle and reattached it to a sturdy iron railing on the pavement. Mrs Hatch had installed it for that very purpose because she greatly disliked animals coming into her shop; she said it wasn't sanitary. Perhaps she was right. In any case, it wasn't wise to leave the dog tethered to the pram, in case he managed to tip it over while lunging at some passing cat.

'Good morning, Nurse! Not bringing young Charlie inside today, then?'

'No, no. It's not all that cold, and he's well wrapped up. I've so many bits and pieces I want to pick up, and it's awkward shopping with a baby on my hip. I could really use three hands instead of two!'

Ever since Mrs Hatch had rearranged her shop to mimic a mini market — moving with the times, she called it — the aisles between the display shelves had been too narrow to accommodate prams. Some mothers had been heard to complain that it had been done on purpose because Mrs Hatch didn't want mud coming in on the pram wheels.

'I suppose there's no news about whoever is trying to bump off Father Christmas, is there, Nurse? The police don't seem to be getting anywhere with that, do they? You ought to have a word with your hubby about it. Ginger him up a bit!'

'I really couldn't say, Mrs Hatch. I don't want to get involved in police matters these days. All my time is taken up with the baby now.'

'That doesn't sound like you, Nurse. Besides, having a baby doesn't stop a woman having an opinion one way or another, does it?'

'I think this is all for now,' Maudie said, emptying her wire basket onto the counter in front of the till. 'Except I seem to have forgotten the cinnamon.'

'Over there, next to the jar of nutmegs.'

At that moment Rover began to bark frantically. 'Now, what's the matter with him?' Mrs Hatch asked, peering out of a side window but unable to see anything.

'Probably a strange cat passing by. He'll calm down as soon as he sees me.'

But when Maudie emerged from the shop, weighed down with a string bag full of last-minute shopping, the dog was still making a fuss.

'Stop that, Rover, do! You're giving me a headache!'

But the dog continued to bark, and when Maudie went to the pram to place her shopping in the luggage compartment, she saw the reason why. Charlie was gone. Turning this way and that, she stared at the deserted street in all directions; but nothing moved, not even a cheeky robin. Clutching her hands to her chest, she began to scream.

Mrs Hatch appeared at the door. 'Whatever's the matter, Nurse? Have you hurt yourself?

'Charlie's gone! Someone's taken my baby!'

'What?'

'Didn't you hear me? My baby's been stolen. Call the police station at Midvale. Don't stand there dithering, woman! Get back in there and call Dick!'

Rover lunged at the end of his leash, still barking hysterically. Maudie, about to release him, thought better of it. If he ran off out of her sight, he might well catch up with the abductor, who could beat him off and escape. She had to keep him with her at all costs. With the leather strap cutting into her palm, she tottered off down the street, towed by the dog.

Shaking her head at the sight, Mrs Hatch peeped into the pram, hoping it was all a mistake. It was true. The baby wasn't there. Feeling lightheaded, she stumbled back into her shop. Was she about to be felled by a stroke? She had to sit down; put her head between her legs.

163

No time for that now. What must she do? Yes! Phone 999. She must get help.

★ ★ ★

At Midvale, Dick Bryant closed his notebook with a groan. With no new leads in sight, the Father Christmas case was going nowhere. There had been no reported attacks on the other three men who were playing the part of the jolly old man from the North Pole, but he had to interview them anyway, just in case the previous muggings had been a case of mistaken identity. What a waste of time that was going to be! If one of the men did have something shady in his background, he wasn't likely to admit it to the police. Still, detective work was all about considering every angle, making sure the pieces of the puzzle fitted together. He slammed his desk drawer shut and went to put on his coat.

He was halfway down the street when he heard shouts coming from the building he had just left. 'Get back here, Bryant! Now!'

'Bad news, I'm afraid,' DI Goodman told him. 'No time to wrap it up nicely, Bryant. We've just had a garbled message from somebody over at Llandyfan. It seems there's been a baby-snatching, and by all accounts it's your son. I'm sorry, lad, but there it is. We'll put extra men on this one, and Joliffe can drive you. No arguments, lad! It won't help your missus if you land in the ditch.'

Maudie! Charlie!

Once in the speeding car, chewing on his nails, Dick glared at his driver. 'Can't this old crate go any faster? Put the siren on, man, for the love of all that's holy!'

'Don't worry, sir. It's probably just a hoax. Some nutter with nothing better to do.'

'Just shut up and drive, will you?'

★　★　★

Maudie sped down the street, hanging onto the leash with all her strength. She felt as if her arm were being dragged out of its socket, but she didn't care. Where was Charlie? Who had taken him? If

Rover was simply following the scent of a car, this could go on for miles. Why, oh why, had she chosen to wear her high heels today, of all days? Please don't let a heel break off! Where was Dick? Had that silly old Hatch woman been in touch? Was he coming? Would he be in time?

They were in sight of the church now, and the nearby graveyard. She pushed away a mental image of her darling baby lying on a tombstone, dead or dying. Who could be so cruel to a poor innocent child?

They were nearing the temporary structure that the churchwardens had put up for the Christmas pageant. Yelping happily, Rover finally succeeded in wrenching himself free and, with his leash trailing behind him, jumped up and peered into the manger. Maudie faltered for a moment, dreading what she might see . . . but then an indignant wail arose and she, too, leapt forward. Tears flooded down her cheeks as she snatched up her son and cradled him in her arms.

Then Joan Blunt was there, placing a comforting arm around her friend's shoulders. 'Is everything all right, Nurse? I've just had the most peculiar conversation with Mrs Hatch. She sounded quite incoherent.'

Maudie gulped. 'This is all wrong.'

'What is?'

'Straw. In the manger. Shouldn't it be hay? Animals don't eat straw, do they?'

'I think you'd better come with me, Nurse. I was about to make myself a cup of tea, and you look as if you could do with one. Here, let me take Charlie. You look quite exhausted.'

'No! You're not having him!' Maudie, clutching her child much too tightly, was not about to let him go, even to a trusted friend.

Joan Blunt had been a vicar's wife for far too long to let this bother her. War, fire, sudden death; her quiet faith enabled her to take everything in her stride. 'That's quite all right, dear. You keep him safe. Just let me take your arm and we'll go inside, shall we? And that dog of yours looks as though he can do with a drink. His tongue is hanging out.'

'Rover is a hero!' Maudie mumbled.

'Of course he is, dear. Now, come along. We don't want Charlie getting cold standing out here.'

'I have to wait for Dick!'

'You can do that in the warm. I'll get Harold to keep a lookout for your husband when he arrives.'

Meekly, Maudie allowed herself to be taken into the vicarage.

19

'Oh, Dick!' Shuddering, Maudie flung herself into her husband's arms. She had let go of Charlie at last, and he lay on the vicarage sofa, safely hemmed in with cushions in case he should roll over and land on the floor.

Dick held her close, whispering words of comfort into her hair. Joan Blunt looked on with approval. She had been aware of a certain coolness between the pair of late, and was happy to see matters resolved now; even though it had taken something horrible like this to bring it about.

'Rover should get a medal,' Maudie said. 'He saved Charlie, you know.'

'Good, good,' Dick said. He could see that the only thing the dog had saved was Maude's sanity: the baby hadn't been harmed, and would have been found sooner or later. Still, if she chose to believe that Rover was their son's guardian angel, so what? She had had a nasty shock, and whatever made her happy was fine with him.

'I left the pram outside the shop, Dick. I must go and fetch it before it rains.'

'The lads will see to all that. Now, shall we get our son home? When we get him down for a nap, I'm afraid I'll have to ask you some questions, just while all this is fresh in your memory.'

Maudie shuddered again. 'Fresh? I don't think I'll ever forget it.'

'Yes, you will, after we've had a chance to talk it all through.'

The walk to their cottage was very different from Maudie's headlong race just a short time before. Quite unaware of the anxiety his parents had felt, Charlie was asleep, slung over his father's shoulder. Rover trotted ahead, stopping now and then to lift his leg against someone's garden gate.

'Herod!' Maudie said suddenly.

'What?'

'You know, in the Bible. King Herod wanted to kill the baby Jesus, so to make sure of it he ordered the killing of all the male infants in and around Bethlehem.'

'Yes?'

'So we've got a Herod here, Dick; some evil person who kidnapped our son. He's got to be stopped before he does it again.'

'I agree he has to be stopped, Maudie, but so far there's nothing to suggest that we have a madman on our hands with plans to kidnap other children. And Charlie is certainly alive and well,' he added, as the baby woke up with a roar of hunger.

'But Charlie may only be alive because Rover took me to him in the nick of time, Dick. Why, the chap could have seen us coming and nipped behind a tombstone before he had the chance to do anything.' The thought of those watching eyes filled Maudie with horror.

* * *

An hour later, Charlie had been fed and put down for a nap. Maudie had been reluctant to leave him alone in his room but Dick, humouring her, had pointed out that the upstairs windows were too small to allow kidnappers to squeeze through; and with half the Midvale police force downstairs, there was no chance of anyone striking again.

'Half the police force' was an exaggeration: Dick and Maudie had now been joined by DI Goodman and a couple of constables who were awaiting further orders.

'Now, then, Mrs Bryant,' Bob Goodman began. 'Shall we run through your story, starting from the moment you left home this morning to go and do your shopping?'

'There's not a lot to tell. I needed a few bits and pieces so I put Charlie in his pram, put Rover on the lead, and off we went.'

'And did you see anybody en route? Anyone loitering near here, let's say?'

She shook her head. 'Only Mrs Cooke up the road, taking in yesterday's washing off the line. Stiff as a board, it was. There really isn't much point hanging things out in this weather. You only have to take it back inside to thaw out.'

'Quite so. And when you arrived at the shop?'

'I didn't see a soul.'

'No cars parked further up the street, perhaps?'

'No. I'm sure there weren't.'

'So you parked the pram outside the shop, tied up your dog, and went inside?'

Maudie looked at Dick. 'I was only gone a few minutes. I thought he'd be safe there. People always leave their children outside in prams, either at the shops or in their own gardens. Nothing like this has ever happened before.'

'Nobody is blaming you, Mrs Bryant. I'm just trying to establish whether this could have been a spur-of-the-moment thing or a premeditated crime,'

'I don't know who from round here would give in to a sudden impulse to snatch a baby,' Maudie said. 'Most people have enough kiddies of their own.'

'A barren woman, longing for a child, perhaps?'

Again Maudie shook her head. 'Not from around here. You forget that I'm a midwife, Mr Goodman. Women talk to me about these things. Even if there was someone who has been unable to conceive, she'd have to be pretty desperate to do a thing like this.'

'But you see, Mrs Bryant, the baby wasn't missing for long. He was simply taken to the church and left safely in the manger. Such a woman could have had a change of heart. She realized the enormity of what she had done, but was took afraid to return your little boy to his pram. So she did the next best thing by leaving him in a safe place where he was certain to be found.'

Dick had been idly looking through a little pile of envelopes he'd picked up from the doormat when they had come into the house. Most seemed to hold Christmas cards, but one cheap white envelope, unstamped, simply bore the name *Bryant* in straggling black letters. He passed it to Goodman.

'Delivered by hand, chief. Could be from our man.'

Opening it carefully, so as to preserve any possible fingerprints, Goodman drew out a torn sheet of lined paper, holding it by one corner. ' 'This is a warning. Keep your nose out or next time the kid dies',' he read aloud.

Maudie stifled a cry. Dick put an arm around her, saying nothing.

'This tells us one thing,' Goodman said. 'Taking Charlie was obviously premeditated. Whoever is responsible must have watched you leaving for work, Bryant, and then waited until your missus left the house.'

'But how could he have known I'd go to the shop this morning? I don't do that every day.'

'Perhaps not, but there would have been another chance. I bet you put the nipper out in the garden for a bit of an airing on a fine day, don't you?'

'In December? Not all that often.'

'But what about when you go out to peg his nappies on the line? Do you always lock the back door behind you?'

'Of course not. But he'd have to get past without me seeing him.'

'Easy enough to whack you over the head, Mrs Bryant. Look, I don't want to alarm you unduly, but we're dealing with a pretty determined person or persons here. Until we catch up with them, you'll have to take extra precautions.'

'Obviously I'm being warned off about something,' Dick said now. 'Could it have anything to do with this Father Christmas business, do you think? I'm to keep my nose out, yet we don't have any major investigations on the go at the moment.'

'Perhaps the warning isn't meant for you at all,' Maudie said. 'Maybe it's directed at me.'

'What are you talking about?'

'The other day, I went over to Brookfield with Cora Beasley. And no, Dick, I haven't been interfering with police business,' she added, seeing Dick's frown. 'I told you about the pregnant teenager who has gone missing.'

'What about her? I told you I went and had a talk with some of the members of that sect in Brookfield, and didn't get anywhere.'

'Cora Beasley employs the girl's father to work at her tree farm, or forestry plantation, whatever you want to call it. She thought it was worth threatening him with the loss of his job if he didn't let his wife search for the girl and bring her home.'

'And what were you doing there, may I ask?'

'As a midwife, to back her up, I suppose.'

'And did this work?'

'Not exactly,' Maudie admitted. 'It seems he'd rather get the sack than abandon his principles.'

'Are you suggesting that this chap kidnapped our son to force you to stay out of his family's business? It sounds pretty far-fetched to me. These people may have some crackpot notions when it comes to religion, but I believe they're a law-abiding bunch as far as it goes.'

'Dick, I haven't had a chance to talk you, but we met another fellow when were there, a labourer of sorts. He was pretty rude to Mrs Beasley, and I'm sure I recognized his voice. He was the man in the Father Christmas costume who got attacked on the night of the party.'

'We already knew about him, love. In fact, I've already been out to the tree farm to talk to him. He might be uncouth, but I doubt very much if he's behind today's business.'

'But don't you see, Dick! He knows about Charlie! I had him with me that day, didn't I? Let's say he really does have something to hide. He gets the wind up when you go to speak to him a second time. So now he's trying to warn you off.'

'Then he's a bigger fool than I took him for. He must know that threatening the police will only make us more determined to get to the bottom of whatever is going on.'

'We must go and have another word with our friend Bracken,' Bob Goodman said. 'I'll handle it myself this time. Not that I don't trust you to do it right, Bryant, but you need to take the rest of the day off to be with your wife. She's had a nasty shock, and I'm sure she'll feel happier to have you close by; just in case this idiot, whoever he is, decides to have another go.'

'It's all right, love. I'll stay here with you. The chief will see to our friend Bracken. If he's the one who took our

Charlie, he'll be behind bars in no time.'

'But what if it wasn't him? What if somebody is still lurking outside, waiting for his chance to . . . '

'Then Rover and I will see him off. I'll take him by the scruff of the neck, and Rover can grab him by the seat of the pants. Between the pair of us, we'll have the handcuffs on him before you can say Herod!'

'Herod?' Goodman queried.

'It's the codename for our new investigation. My wife came up with it. Operation Herod! You know, he was the wicked king who tried to kill the baby Jesus.'

'Thank you, Bryant! I went to Sunday School as well, you know.'

'Yes, sir. Of course you did.'

In spite of the worry that weighed her down like a huge black summer thundercloud, Maudie managed to smile. Their dog had already proved his worth today, and she and Dick were all right again.

20

'It's all right, love. The chap's gone, and he won't be coming back.' Dick rubbed Maudie's back gently as the pair of them stood looking down at their sleeping son.

'You can't know that, Dick! I want you to move the cot into our room. The baby will sleep with us from now on.'

'Come on, old girl; that's going a bit far. We'll leave both bedroom doors open, and that should be good enough. Or do you want me to sleep on the floor so that anybody trying to get into Charlie's room will fall over me and knock himself out?'

'It's nothing to joke about,' Maudie protested, but she managed a smile. Herod, as she now thought of the kidnapper, might well be far away by now, but how did they know he'd been acting alone? He might be part of a gang.

'I don't think I'll get a wink of sleep,'

she went on. 'I might sit up for a bit. I'll camp out in the rocking chair beside the cot.'

'This isn't like the Maudie I know and love,' Dick said. 'You've always had the willpower of a lion, facing down thieves and murderers. Why, it takes tremendous courage to bring babies into the world, all alone, and sometimes under difficult circumstances. You mustn't give way to fear now.'

'It's easy to find courage for oneself,' Maudie told him. 'In the face of danger you just pull yourself together, take a deep breath, and face up to whatever may come. Now I'm a mother, it's different. I'd die to save Charlie — but what if I don't have the strength, Dick? If anything happened to that little boy, I'd die. I just know I would.'

'We'll have no silly talk about dying, thank you very much! But it wouldn't hurt to call up the reinforcements.'

'I don't know what you mean.'

Dick grinned. He went to the head of the staircase and whistled. Rover shot up the stairs and into the baby's room, where he threw himself down under the cot, panting.

'On guard, boy! Stay!'

'A fat lot of good he'll be,' Maudie said, laughing. 'If an intruder breaks in, that dog is likely to roll over on his back with his paws waving,'

'Oh no, Maudie. He's seen Herod off once today, and I've no doubt that he'll do it again if necessary; which it won't be. Now, are you coming to bed or not? I'm getting cold standing here half-dressed.'

Lying in the warmth of her husband's arms, Maudie slept fitfully. At times her thoughts went back to the war years, when Britons and the Empire had stood alone against the forces of evil. They had daily expected the invasion to take place, and she had often wondered how she would react if jackbooted men strutted down the village street, killing and looting. She liked to think that she would join a resistance movement in the Welsh mountains, although perhaps she wouldn't have been given the chance. She was more likely to find herself in a prison camp, where she would use her nursing skills to assist other women inmates.

'Oh, do stop this, you fool!' Maudie said aloud. 'It never happened, and nothing is going to happen now! Get to sleep and stop fussing.'

'Who? What?' Dick struggled to sit up.

'It's all right,' she whispered. 'Go back to sleep.'

Dick grunted and rolled over, taking most of the bedclothes with him. Maudie yanked them back.

★　★　★

In the clear light of morning, her fears receded as she busied herself with her usual tasks. There was Dick's breakfast to be cooked and served, and Charlie to be fed and changed. Her heart skipped a beat when a loud clanking came from the scullery, but it was only Rover making his presence felt. He appeared in the kitchen doorway, holding his enamel bowl in his teeth. Maudie took it from him and filled it with dry dog food, which he sniffed at and rejected. There were sausages in the frying pan, and he knew it!

'I must be off,' Dick said at last. 'I want to see what's been going on at the station. I expect they've caught Herod by now.'

'As soon as you know anything, do call and let me know,' Maudie pleaded. 'I shan't have a moment's peace until I know he's behind bars.'

'I'll try; but will you be in all day, love?'

'I don't see why not. One of your chaps delivered the shopping I had to leave behind when I ran off looking for Charlie. I've no need to go outside at all. I think I'll have a nice quiet day at home.'

'Whatever you say, love.'

As soon as she heard Dick's car driving off, Maudie flew into action. Having locked the front door and put on the chain, testing it twice to make sure it was secure, she raced to the back door, where she tested the bolt. Next, she checked that all the windows were firmly closed, and for good measure she lifted the telephone receiver off its cradle and listened to make sure that the instrument was working.

Once she had attended to the baby, she

sat down at the table to address some Christmas cards. After a moment, she got up and went to fetch her heavy wooden rolling pin. She had never been a Girl Guide, but she approved of their motto. Be Prepared! Comforted, she picked up her fountain pen and began to write.

★   ★   ★

It was almost lunchtime, and Dick hadn't phoned. Surely he hadn't forgotten? He knew how worried she was. Maudie picked up the receiver again. The line was still working. The wires had not been cut by Herod or his henchmen.

Rover went to the door and whined. 'I suppose I'll have to let you out, old boy,' she told him. 'No W-A-L-K for you today, I'm afraid.' Clever though the animal was, he had not yet learned to spell! She dared not mention the word in his hearing, for it would send him into a frenzy of joyful barking. She let him out through the scullery door, shooting the bolt home immediately.

Rover was not a dog who went

walkabout as soon as he was released outdoors. She expected that he would gratefully relieve himself against the gatepost — just to confirm his territory in case any strange dog came wandering by — and then spend a few minutes sniffing about in the back garden. After that, he would scratch at the back door, wanting to return to the warmth of his bed in the scullery.

His wild yelping gave her pause. At one time such a display would have heralded the intrusion of Perkin, the vicarage cat, but the two were firm friends now. Perhaps a stray was passing by and Rover was warning it off?

The yelps turned into a loud, shrill barking. This was something more than an encounter between two household pets. Sadly, there were no windows on that side of the cottage, so Maudie couldn't see what was happening. Her only choice was to open the back door and look out, but she wasn't that much of a fool!

Grasping the rolling pin, she darted to the front door. She had a key in her apron pocket; she could step outside, closing the door behind her, and tiptoe round the side of the house to see what was up with Rover.

But, just as she was attempting to steel herself into action, the letterbox rattled. Somebody was out there! She waited. If a shower of post came through the door, it would signal the arrival of Bert Harvey, their postman. Right! She would whip the door open and ask Bert to come and help her investigate.

Under her terrified gaze, a single cheap white envelope fell onto the mat. From where she stood, she could see the straggly black lettering on the front.

21

'We've lost him. He's flown the coop.' DI Goodman explained when Dick reported for duty that morning. 'We went over to the farm right after we left your place yesterday, but Croome told us the chap hadn't reported for work that day. That proves nothing, of course, though it does mean he would have been free to go to Llandyfan. He doesn't run a car, but it would have been easy enough to get the bus over, or even to thumb a lift.'

'What about his home?'

'The place was deserted. We quizzed the neighbours, but no joy there. They all say he kept himself to himself. Didn't even drink at the local pub.'

'So either they know nothing, or they're not saying.' Dick said. 'What about his landlord?'

'Landlady. A widow woman who lived there herself until her husband died. Now she lives with her married daughter down by the mill. According to her, he's not behind with the rent; and while he doesn't do much to keep the property up, at least he doesn't do any damage around the place. It seems our Bracken is a model citizen, Bryant.'

'Maudie doesn't trust him.'

'Come on, Bryant! Women's intuition has no place in police work, as you ought to know. Besides, after what happened between the chap and your missus the night of the party, it's no wonder she feels awkward around him.'

'I suppose so. The fact remains that she had a terrible shock yesterday — we both did — when our Charlie was taken. Neither of us will rest easy until we get the man responsible for that.'

'Or woman.'

'What makes you believe it was a woman?'

'I don't. But then there's nothing to say it was a man, either.'

Dick glared at his boss. 'You'll forgive me for saying so, sir, but I feel you're taking this much too lightly! My son was stolen from his pram yesterday, and all you can say is that you don't know whether he was taken by a man or a woman! What about that note we found? It's obvious to me that this is connected with some big crime we're not aware of yet. Somebody has been watching my house and checking on my wife's movements, and it has to stop!' Dick thumped on the desk with his fist. Tea splashed out of his cup, leaving wet blotches on the papers nearby.

'Calm down, Bryant! The main thing is that the nipper was returned unharmed.'

'Only because of my dog!'

'That's a matter of opinion. I don't believe that the kidnapper intended any harm to come to your boy. He just wanted to draw attention to his demands, whatever they may be.'

'He did that all right!'

'Yes, well, rest assured that I've put every available man on the job.'

'And will you be putting a guard on my home, sir? My wife is as jittery as a bee in a bottle. She has to know that what took place yesterday can't happen again.'

'I'll tell you what I'll do, Bryant. This

case is too close to you; understandably so. You must leave the rest of us to handle it. Why not take compassionate leave and stay home with your wife and son?'

'Oh, no, sir! Absolutely not! I want to see this case through to the end.'

'And what will you do when you catch up with the chap, Bryant? See red, and give him the old one-two? Perhaps kill him and get yourself up on a charge of manslaughter? I don't think so. You'll go on paid leave for an indefinite period, Bryant. Starting now!'

★ ★ ★

Maudie waited. Rover continued to bark hysterically. The footsteps receded, and the barks grew fainter. Shaking, she staggered to the table and sat down heavily. It seemed that Rover had chased the intruder away — for now — or had at least followed him off the premises. She feared for the dog's safety, but there was nothing she could do about that.

The front door rattled again and she jumped up, grasping the rolling pin.

'It's all right, love. Only me!'

'Dick! It's you!'

'Of course it's me! Who did you think it was, Father Christmas?' As soon as the words were out of his mouth, Dick realized that his joke had fallen flat. His wife burst into tears and hurled herself into his arms.

'Shut the door, Dick! For goodness' sake, lock the door! He might come back!'

'Did someone show up here? Who was it, love? Was it Bracken?'

'I don't know!' she sobbed. 'But he put that note through the letterbox.'

'What does it say?'

'How do I know? I didn't open the beastly thing.'

Dick tore the envelope open and extracted a scrap of lined paper.

Next time the kid dies.

'Is it another threat?'

He nodded. 'Same as before, love. Well, whoever he is, he should be happy now. I've been taken off the case.'

Maudie's eyes opened wide. 'Don't tell me you've been suspended!'

'No, no. The chief's making me take compassionate leave. I think he's afraid that if I catch up with whoever snatched Charlie, I'll do him a mischief — and he's not far wrong, at that!'

'Then you'll be able to stay home with us? Oh, I'm so glad!' Maudie pulled a soaking handkerchief out of her apron pocket as the tears began to flow again.

'What's Charlie up to?' Dick asked. 'Asleep, is he?'

'Safe and sound upstairs,' Maudie replied.

'And what about the Hound of the Baskervilles? He's up there too, is he?'

Maudie gulped. 'That poor dog! I'd forgotten about him for a minute. I let him out to do his business, and he went mad, barking at the intruder. Of course, I didn't realize that at the time, not until that note came through the door. Then he disappeared, still yelping, and I assume he went after the chap. I can't imagine where he's got to.'

Moments later, she breathed a sigh of relief when they heard a scratching at the back door, followed by a soft whine. Their dog came inside limping, with his tail between his legs, but he submitted to Maudie's anxious probing without fuss.

'I don't think he's been hurt,' she said at last.

'Probably just exhausted from chasing after chummy. The bloke may have had a bike or a van parked around the corner, ready for a quick getaway.'

'My hero!' Maudie sighed.

'Who, me? Well, I do my best!'

'Not you, you fool! Wouldums like a cold sausage, then?' she cooed.

'Arf!' said Rover.

★　★　★

'So what do we do next, then?' Maudie asked. It was late that evening, and they were relaxing in their favourite armchairs in front of the fire. Charlie had been put to bed at his usual time, and the loyal Rover had accompanied the baby to the nursery.

A piece of coal fell onto the hearth, making Maudie jump. She had closed the living room curtains as carefully as she had always arranged them during war-time nights. In fact, she heartily wished that she still had the hated blackout drapes, which would have prevented anyone from seeing in.

'I think you should go away for a while,' Dick began.

'Go away? What do you mean?'

'Just until this business is settled, love.'

'But where would I go? All the boarding houses will be closed for the winter, and even if we could afford a hotel, they'll all be chockablock with Christmas coming.'

'Don't you have any family some-where?'

She rolled her eyes at him. 'You know I don't, and neither do you.'

'Friends, then. Aren't you still in touch with some of your old nursing col-leagues?'

'Of course I am, but I'm not about to inflict myself on any of them for Christmas; especially with a baby, Dick Bryant.'

'I'm sure if they knew the reason they'd be more than glad to give you shelter.'

'No, Dick, and that's an end to it! If you think I'm going to let this Herod creature drive me out of my own home, away from my husband, with Christmas almost upon us, you've got another think coming. Hitler didn't manage to put us on the run, so I don't see why we should let some petty crook dictate to us.'

'Very well, but if you're going to stay we'll have to establish some ground rules.'

Another coal dropped from the fire and this time Maudie managed not to flinch. 'What rules? I don't know what else we can do. We're already under siege here, and I'm jolly well not going out again unless you're with us.'

'Rule number one. We won't give any interviews to the press.'

'Of course not. Why would we?'

'Obviously you haven't seen today's *Midvale Chronicle*. I wasn't going to show you this, but I suppose you'd better have a look at it before someone else spills the beans.' He reached into his briefcase and handed her a newspaper, folded open to reveal an article headed with bold black type. Maudie stared at it in dismay.

Baby Snatched at Llandyfan. Child's Life Threatened.

'Where did they get hold of this rubbish? How could they print something like this?'

Dick shrugged. 'I suppose you can't blame them. It's the sort of story that sells newspapers. Detective's son snatched under the noses of the police. Innocent child in danger, and all that rot.'

'But it's *our* innocent child that's in danger, Dick, and I want to know who gave this story to the press!'

'I think if you turn to page seven you'll see for yourself, love.'

And there, on page seven, was a simpering image of their village postmistress, complete with a highly embroidered story. '*I was on the spot when it happened,*' says Vera Hatch, 59. '*I witnessed the mother's anguish when her little boy was torn from her bosom. It was I who called 999 to bring Detective Sergeant Dick Bryant to his wife's aid.*'

'I'll swing for that woman!' Maudie howled. 'Torn from my bosom, indeed! And she makes it sound as though she single-handedly saved Charlie, when she didn't move from her shop! Oh, just you wait until I see that woman again! I'll give her what for! And she's such a hypocrite, Dick. Just the other day she warned me against ever giving an interview to the papers, but now it's a different story when she can hog the limelight.'

'Funny, that,' Dick murmured. 'I'd have said she was much older than fifty-nine, wouldn't you?'

'She is!' Maudie retorted. 'I know for a fact she's seventy-three!'

'Really? Are you sure?'

'Absolutely!' his wife replied, crossing her fingers behind her back.

22

'I need a haircut,' Dick said, 'so I suppose I'd better take a jaunt into Midvale. Do you want to come along?'

'Well, if you think I'm staying here alone, you've got another think coming, Dick Bryant! What about those ground rules you were so keen on, eh?'

'Just checking!'

'I could always cut it for you, I suppose,' Maudie suggested.

'Not on your life! If the result was anything like that pudding-basin trim you've given our son, people would assume I've just been released from prison!'

'Charlie looks the way he does because I don't have much to work with! Some children come out of the womb with a full head of hair, but he is one of those babies whose locks take time to grow.'

'If you say so. Well then, get your coat on and we'll set off.'

But the days were gone when Maudie could be ready to leave after tugging a comb through her own hair and putting on a smear of lipstick. Charlie had had his morning bath, but he still needed to be changed, dressed in warm clothes, and his mother had to make sure that the ever-present nappy bag contained all the items of infant gear to suit every eventuality. It wasn't long before Dick was standing at the foot of the stairs, drumming his fingers on the newel post.

'What's going on up there, Maudie? I could have gone there and back by now!'

'Hold your horses, will you? If I leave him in these wet pants, he'll bawl all the way to Midvale and back!'

Dick sighed, and looked at his wristwatch again.

At long last, they were on their way, Dick driving and Maudie in the passenger seat with the baby on her lap.

'I noticed a sale of Christmas trees in the market square the other day, old girl. Should we get one? That's if they haven't already been snapped up.'

'Yes, I'd love one.'

'What size, then? One to stand on the floor, or a miniature one for the table?'

Maudie thought for a moment. 'Let's go all out with an enormous one that almost touches the ceiling.'

'Any particular reason?'

Maudie smiled. 'This time next year, Charlie boy will be crawling all over the place, possibly even walking. We can't risk him pulling the tree down on top of himself, so it will have to be table trees for the next few years.'

'True enough. Well, here we are at the barber's; and wonder of wonders, a spare parking spot. What are you going to do while I'm in there?'

'I'll go into Woolworth's and see if I can lay my hands on a few decorations. You come and find us there when you've finished.'

'Right ho!'

But, as it happened, Dick, sporting his new short-back-and-sides, decided to look at the trees first. Several other men were doing the same thing, so that when he had made his selection he wasn't sure who was meant to be taking his money.

'Can I help you, sir?'

The man at his elbow looked vaguely familiar. Where had he seen him before? In the ironmonger's, perhaps? He was dressed in a brown shop coat over an ancient suit, and around his waist he wore one of those aprons designed for holding nails or stowing away the money spent on fairground rides.

Then everything fell into place. 'Aren't you Alfred Morton?'

'Who wants to know?'

'DS Bryant, Midvale police.'

'I ain't doing nothing wrong.'

'Nobody says you are. I just wondered how you were feeling after your bump on the head.'

'I ain't felt right since. And I wish you coppers would leave me alone. Isn't it bad enough I've lost my job, on account of being falsely accused of something I never done, without this never-ending hounding? I've got to make a living somehow, and I'm too proud to go on the social, so here I am, see?'

'Very commendable, I'm sure. And I'm not here to check up on you. I just want a nice tree for my family. Where did these come from, anyway? Scotland, perhaps, or Norway?'

'Don't ask me, mate! I only sell them.' He took the money Dick held out, and turned to serve another customer.

⋆ ⋆ ⋆

Maudie was delighted with the tree. They drove home singing, the tree on the back seat of the car with its tip poking out through the window.

'Let's hope this tree isn't dodgy,' Dick muttered. 'Wouldn't it be wonderful if I was found to be receiving stolen goods?'

'Dodgy? Why should it be?'

'Only that the salesman happens to be Alf Morton. That's the first Father Christmas who was coshed over the head.'

'But surely he was the chap who stole all that stuff from the post office? Why isn't he in prison?'

'He's out on bail because we couldn't prove anything against him. He's still claiming amnesia as a result of the attack, and we can't beat a confession out of him, more's the pity.'

'But all that stuff that was found in his home? That's evidence, surely?'

'He claims he was framed. By whom, and for what reason, is far from clear. All that is lost in the mists of his amnesia. Mind you, his dabs aren't on any of it, so who knows? He could be telling the truth.'

★　★　★

If Maudie was delighted with their purchase, Rover was ecstatic. He sniffed madly at the tree, identifying the scents of people or animals who had previously handled it. Dick propped it up in the corner, saying he would wire it to the wall for safety just as soon as they had found a suitable pail to stand it in.

'Rover! Don't you dare!' Maudie spoke in the nick of time when she caught sight of him cocking his leg against the tree trunk. The dog slunk under the table, ashamed. 'You're supposed to be house-trained!' she scolded.

'I expect he's only trying to establish his territory,' Dick said. 'Dogs do that when they feel threatened.'

'He'll feel threatened if he tries that again,' Maudie retorted. 'I'm having no dirty dogs in my house.' She bent down and glared at the dog. 'Dogs who lift their legs inside the house have to live in the scullery. Do you understand?'

He moaned unhappily, causing her to relent. This was the animal who had saved Charlie, and then driven the intruder away a second time. Rover was a hero!

'All right, good dog! You can come out now. Just stay away from that tree; do you understand?'

Later that evening, Maudie and Dick looked at their tree with satisfaction. It might not have won any prizes for decoration, but it looked cheerful enough, draped in tinsel and displaying a few precious ornaments Maudie had kept for years. Somehow it spoke of home, and love, and tradition. Illuminated by the flickering light of the fire on the hearth, it transformed the room from the commonplace into the magical.

'I wish we had a string of fairy lights, though,' she murmured. 'I still think it looks a bit bare, don't you?'

'Just wait till we get our presents stacked up underneath it, then it will look okay. Besides, I don't know as I hold with fairy lights indoors. Somehow they seem too modern, and nothing much to do with Christmas. Didn't they use lighted candles on their trees in the old days?'

Maudie shuddered. 'And I wonder how many folk found themselves homeless as a result? We'll have none of that, thank you! It's a shame though that we'll have to get rid of the tree when the needles begin to drop. What shall we do with it?'

'We'll stick it in the ground and decorate it with bits of suet for the birds,' said practical Dick.

'Oh, yes? And attract all the cats in the neighbourhood?'

'Who cares?' Dick replied. 'Rover will see them off, won't you, boy?'

'Arf!' said Rover.

23

'I'm going to pop over and see Cora Beasley,' Maudie announced, peering out of the window to find that the sun was shining on the frosty ground

'You're doing what?'

'You heard me.'

'I may have heard you, but I don't like what I hear, Maudie Bryant! Just how do you propose to get there?'

'On my bike, of course.'

'And what's to stop someone catching up with you and pulling you off it? Perhaps running you down with a car? You know what we said.'

'All right, all right! Come with me, then, if you're so worried.'

Nothing untoward had happened over the past few days, and Maudie was beginning to chafe at the unprecedented confinement to home. The man who had threatened them was far away by now; he wouldn't dare to strike again while Dick was at home with her.

Dick, on the other hand, was an experienced police officer who knew that where criminal activity was concerned, nothing could ever be taken for granted. Herod was probably just biding his time and would strike again in due course. He sighed.

'All right, we'll all go. Rover can come along as well, and I'll give him a run in Mrs Beasley's grounds while you two are having your chinwag. I'm sure she won't mind. But do telephone first and make sure she's at home.'

Maudie made several attempts to contact Mrs Beasley, only to get the engaged tone each time. Finally, she insisted that they set out, or Charlie's daily schedule would be seriously disrupted before they got very far.

'I've been trying to contact you, Detective Sergeant Bryant,' Mrs Beasley exclaimed when she saw who was standing on her doorstep. 'But the line was always engaged.'

'That's because my wife was trying to telephone to you!' Dick said. 'Is there something wrong, Mrs Beasley?'

'I'm afraid there is, but I mustn't keep you standing on the doorstep in this cold, it isn't good for young Charlie! Do come in! Bring the dear little doggie with you.'

They followed her into the morning room, where the first few moments were taken up in the rituals of hospitality. Would they like to join her in a cup of coffee? Yes, they would. Would Rover like a bikkie? Arf, said the dear little doggie. He was rather partial to the Marie biscuits he sometimes received from the lady of the manor.

'Well, it's like this, Mr Bryant,' Mrs Beasley began when they were settled. 'I had a visit from an old friend yesterday. Actually, we were at school together, not that that has anything to do with what I'm trying to tell you. She and her son were just passing through, and they stopped by to say hello. We got talking, the way you do, and it transpires that the son has a small estate on which he's thinking of planting conifers.'

'Go on.'

'So, of course I said that if they had

time he should pop over to Brookfield and have a look at my plantation. He could get some idea of the space needed, and so on. He seemed quite keen to do that, so we decided that Jean should stay on with me while he nipped over to Brookfield. When he returned, he told me that a large section of the plantation had apparently been cut down, with just the stumps remaining. I don't like the sound of this, Mr Bryant. I don't like it at all.'

'Isn't it possible that your foresters, or whatever you call them, have been doing some routine pruning or culling, perhaps?'

'Hardly! The trees do have to be limbed, of course, but I certainly haven't authorized any clear-cutting.'

'When we visited your farm, you mentioned that the trees sometimes have to be sprayed against pests in the spring,' Maudie said. 'Perhaps a section of trees was somehow missed, and now they have died and been removed?'

'I suppose it's possible.' Mrs Beasley sounded doubtful.

'Why don't I take a run over there and

have a look?' Dick suggested.

'I'd be pleased if you would. But I've been monopolizing the conversation, and you haven't had a chance to explain why you wished to see me.'

'I wondered if you'd heard anything more about Lily Rose,' Maudie said. 'The child must be so close to her time, and I can't bear to think of her giving birth all alone, terrified and in grave danger.'

'I'm afraid I've rather let things slide,' Mrs Beasley admitted. 'This is such a busy time of year, and my chauffeur has been down with a nasty cold and unable to drive me anywhere. I haven't done anything about sacking the girl's father, though. I didn't think that was right, not at Christmastime. So I decided to forget about him until the New Year.'

'Then I'll go with Dick and see if I can browbeat Croome into telling me if he knows where his daughter can be found. For all we know, he could have the girl locked in the attic so she doesn't disgrace him by appearing heavily pregnant in front of the neighbours.'

Mrs Beasley glanced at Charlie, who

was beginning to stir. 'It's a cold day to go tramping all over the countryside with a young child in tow. Why don't you leave the baby with me while you're gone? I'd love to have the little chap.'

'Oh, no, we couldn't do that,' Maudie said at once. 'It's a very kind offer, but we wouldn't dream of imposing.'

Cora Beasley patted Maudie's hand. 'I think I know why you don't wish to leave Charlie here, Nurse. Quite naturally you're a little frightened, under the circumstances. But my maid and I will take good care of him, and we'll keep the doors firmly shut and locked, and nobody will know that he's even here. Rover can stay for extra protection.'

After a nod from Dick, Maudie reluctantly agreed to the plan, handing over the tapestry bag that contained the baby's bits and pieces. 'There's a bottle here that just needs heating up; you can give him that if he wakes. And a change of clothes, and half a dozen nappies.'

'Goodness, you have come well pre-pared!'

'Yes, well, there's nothing wrong with

the little tinker's bladder. He lives to make washing for his poor old mum, don't you, Charlie Bryant?' She touched the baby lovingly, beaming down on him when his tiny fingers curled around her forefinger.

★ ★ ★

'I have a nasty idea that somehow this all fits together,' Dick muttered as he drove along the deserted lanes towards Brookfield.

'What, exactly?'

'Right now, the missing trees and the fact that Samuel Bracken, alias Father Christmas, has gone AWOL. And if my suspicions are right, he and Morton are somehow connected; and from there, it follows that you and I are in possession of stolen goods!'

'We'd better have a look at the plantation before you jump to any conclusions,' Maudie warned. But when they had hiked for some distance, finishing up at a part of the farm not visible from the entrance yard, it was plain that some skulduggery had been at work. A whole section of trees was missing, and it hadn't happened naturally.

'They've all been neatly sawn off,' Dick observed as he bent to examine the remaining stumps. 'And judging by the surrounding trees, these were just the right size for use as Christmas trees in the home.'

'So you're probably right about those trees being sold at Midvale.'

'These blokes had it made, didn't they? Everyone knows that Cora Beasley hires them to work here, so if their comings and goings were observed, nobody would think anything of it. Even if the trees were seen being loaded onto a lorry, people would assume that it was on her authority.'

'It was rather bold of them to sell them at Midvale, though, don't you think? And wouldn't they need a vendor's permit to set up shop in the square?'

'They would indeed, and that will have to be looked into. Meanwhile I want to have a look in that hut, just in case any of the crooks are lurking inside.'

'Is it worth it? Nobody came out when we drove in.'

I'll check it out anyway.'

But when Dick approached the hut with Maudie in tow, the first thing he noticed was a large padlock holding the door firmly shut. 'There may be another way in,' he said, pushing his way through a bank of dying nettles to get to the rear of the dilapidated building. 'No joy,' he called, reappearing from the other side.

But Maudie's senses were on high alert and she held up a warning finger. 'Do stop crashing about like that, Dick! I'm sure I heard something. Hark! There it is again! Someone is in there, and by the sound of it he's been hurt. We've got to get this door open, and be quick about it.'

24

'Are you sure? I can't hear anything.'
Dick stumbled towards his wife, suppressing a curse as a wayward bramble tore a
painful scratch in his hand. 'Are you sure
you didn't imagine it? Perhaps it was the
wind lifting a loose board or something,
making it squeal.'

'I heard something, I know I did; but
it's quiet now.'

'If there *is* somebody inside, they
certainly couldn't have locked themselves
in with a padlock on the outside. Perhaps
it's a case of a falling-out among thieves!
Ivan Croome sees what Bracken is up to,
threatens to go to Mrs Beasley, and he
gets walloped for his pains and left for
dead.'

'There it is again!' Maudie said. 'For
goodness' sake, Dick; get a move on,
can't you?'

'Hang on while I get a tyre iron out of
the boot.'

'And fetch a torch while you're about it!' she called after him.

* * *

The single window the hut possessed was too dirty to permit much light to enter. Straining her eyes against the gloom, Maudie peered into the dark recesses of the foresters' shelter. Something stirred and moaned on the floor in the corner. She dropped her knees beside the writhing figure, beckoning to Dick to come closer with the torch.

'Who are you? Get away from me!' The young girl shrank closer to the wall, raising an arm to shield her eyes from the light.

'It's quite all right, dear. You're quite safe with me. I'm Nurse Bryant, and I'm here to help you. And I believe you are Lily Rose Croome; am I right?'

'How do you know my name? Did my dad send you?'

'We haven't seen your father today, although we had expected to find him here. Do you know where he might be?'

'He may be at the hospital by now. Mum said he'd ruptured himself. He didn't want to go, on account of he doesn't hold with doctors, but she said the way he was carrying on, roaring and throwing himself about, she might have to ring 999 anyway and suffer the consequences later.'

'And that's where you should be as well, young lady,' Dick said.

'No!' the girl screamed. 'You can't make me! You don't know him! He'll harm my baby, I know he will!'

'Nonsense!' Maudie snapped. 'If the man has a hernia, he's either recovering from an operation or he's in no condition to do harm to anyone. Now then, let me take a look at you. I'm a midwife, so I know what I'm doing. Dick, bring that light closer, please.'

'We passed a telephone box at the crossroads,' Dick said when Maudie had conducted her examination of the patient. 'I'll drive back and phone for an ambulance, shall I?'

'Too late for that. The baby is about to crown, and I can't manage without light.

We'll have to do the best we can, that's all.'

'What does that mean?' the girl gasped. 'Is there something wrong with the baby? Am I going to die? Oh, I want my mum!'

'All is well,' Maudie assured her. 'I was just telling my husband that the baby's head will appear in a minute, and after that it won't be long before he or she comes safely into the world. Yes, I know it hurts, dear; I'm a mother myself and I know all about it! But if you'll just do exactly what I tell you, it will soon be over. Can you manage that?'

Lily Rose nodded and screamed. Maudie glanced at Dick over her shoulder. 'As soon as the baby is delivered, I want you to nip out to the car and fetch my handbag.'

Dick nodded. 'Anything else?'

'We don't have anything else. Unfortunately, I didn't bring my midwifery bag; but never mind, we'll just have to make do.'

Maudie continued with the task in hand, working more by feel than anything else. 'Give me one big push now, Lily

Rose, and the worse will be over.'

'I can't! I can't!'

'You can, and you will. Give her your hand, Dick, and let her squeeze it.'

Crouching in the dark, with one hand on the patient and the other trying to keep the torch still, Dick winced but played his part manfully. The baby slid into the world, complaining loudly.

'No need to smack this one's bottom,' Maudie observed. 'You have a lovely little girl, Lily Rose.'

'Can I see her? Can I hold her?'

'Of course you can. Open my bag, Dick, and pass me my scissors so I can deal with the cord. They're not sterile, but that can't be helped. And there should be a bit of string in there as well. Luckily, I kept forgetting to take it out!'

'She's so beautiful!' the young mother breathed. 'But I don't have a stitch to put on her. What are we going to do?'

'Not to worry. My husband is going to sacrifice his nice clean hanky, aren't you, love?'

It was a standing joke between Maudie and Dick that he favoured extra-large cotton squares because they were useful for more than blowing his nose! By tying knots in each of the four corners, he could fashion a useful hat for protection against the sun; while, in a pinch, a large hanky could be used in any number of first aid procedures.

'And if you look in my handbag again, you'll find a couple of large safety pins.' During the war it had been almost impossible to buy elastic, and Maudie had dreaded the thought of her underwear letting her down at an inopportune moment. She remembered the day when she had been out with a number of nursing colleagues, crossing a busy street, when one of the girls had let out a shriek of dismay.

'It's my knicker elastic!' she hissed. The group had immediately surrounded their distressed friend, shielding her from public view while she stepped out of the offending garment. Gales of laughter accompanied her hasty stuffing of a handful of pink crêpe de chine into her coat pocket. Maudie had learned a lesson from this, and had carried safety pins on her person ever since, just in case. Now they enabled her to pin Dick's spotted hankie into an impromptu nappy on Baby Girl Croome.

'And we'll wrap her in this very nice blanket you had lying over you,' she went on.

'Mum brought that for me. She didn't want me getting cold, she said.'

'Now shall I phone for an ambulance?' Dick asked.

'I think, if you can manage to carry Lily Rose to the car, we'll take her to the cottage hospital ourselves.'

'But what if Dad's there?' Lily Rose quavered.

'That's precisely why I want to go there. I shall have a few home truths to share with that gentleman.'

With Lily Rose and her baby installed in the back seat, they set off, with Maudie hanging over the back of the passenger seat to keep an eye on her patients. On her lap she held a rather grisly memento of their experience, in the form of the afterbirth held in a wartime relic. The tin helmet must have belonged to some member of the Home Guard who for some reason had kept watch in the hut in the days when invasion by the enemy was expected daily. It was important that the afterbirth should be carefully examined to make sure that no pieces of tissue had been left inside the mother, where it could lead to a haemorrhage. The tin hat being the only receptacle available, it would have to do.

'I want to call the baby after you, Nurse,' Lily Rose said sleepily. 'What is your Christian name?'

Maudie had received this honour more than once before, so she knew how to reply. 'It's Maudie. Well, I was christened Maud, but I've never actually been called that. Not many babies are given that name today, so if you really mean what you say, perhaps you might prefer my middle name, Grace.'

'Grace. Yes, I like the sound of that.' Lily Rose kissed her baby on the forehead. 'Did you hear that, little one? Grace. Your name is Grace.'

★　★　★

'Mum! Mum!' Lily Rose, sitting in a wheelchair with Grace on her lap, was being transported down the hospital corridor by a nurse in a green smock when she spied her mother lingering outside the door of the male surgical ward.

'Lily Rose! How did you get here? What's happened?' Mrs Croome's mouth dropped open when she saw the bundle on her daughter's lap. 'Is it the baby? Is it all right? How did you manage?'

'We can't stop here,' the nurse said officiously. 'We've got to get this baby examined. You can talk to your mother later.'

'Speak to Nurse Bryant, Mum,' Lily Rose called, as she was whisked away.

'Nurse Bryant,' Mrs Croome muttered. 'I might have known she'd have something to do with it.'

25

Sitting in a hospital waiting room, fortunately deserted, Maudie and the new grandmother exchanged words while Dick sat silently by.

'Tell me everything,' Maudie insisted. 'How did you find Lily Rose? And why on earth lock her up in the foresters' hut? Was it some sort of punishment?'

'No, of course it wasn't. I had to protect her, didn't I?'

'So?'

'Well, I found out that she'd gone to our Edna, my hubby's sister in Oxford. She didn't let us know at first because she was afraid of what he might do, but then her hubby was due home from a business trip, bringing a mate with him on a promised visit, and she didn't have the room to keep Lily on. So she got in touch with me in secret. I had to pretend that Edna had asked me to stay for the weekend to help her get ready for Harry's friend. Well, it wasn't a lie, really; she *had* asked me to go there, hadn't she?'

'So you brought Lily Rose back to Brookfield.'

'Only I couldn't have her to the house, or Ivan would have cut up rough. Well, he was already in pain with his rupture, and I knew he couldn't go back to work, so I hid Lily in the hut. I locked her in, but I didn't leave her unattended. I went back every day and took her food and that.'

'But how did you know that Bracken wouldn't come across her there, Mrs Croome?' Dick interrupted, speaking for the first time.

'Sam? Oh, he's gone to Banbury, hasn't he? He won't be coming back. Not if he knows what's good for him.'

'Banbury!' Dick said thoughtfully. 'Perhaps you'd better tell me the whole story, Mrs Croome.'

*   *   *

'And that's the story,' Dick concluded, when they had filled Mrs Beasley in on the whole sorry affair. After leaving the hospital, he and Maudie had sped back to Llandyfan to retrieve Charlie and Rover, where they had found that all was well.

'So what you are telling me is, this Bracken fellow has been cutting down my trees to sell for his own profit!' she said. 'And you say that Croome knew all about it and covered up for him, instead of coming to me. And to think I took pity on the man when I should have sacked him!'

'Ah, but he's been well punished,' Maudie reminded her. 'He ruptured himself trying to lift a piece of fallen masonry at the back of his cottage, and his wife managed to convince him that it was a judgement on him for his sins. Not only was he protecting Bracken from the law, he had also turned his daughter out of their home, which in his wife's eyes was a far worse crime. She finally talked him into seeing a doctor, although my guess is that she wanted him out of the way for Lily Rose's sake rather than from any sympathy towards him.'

'And you say he's at the cottage hospital now?'

'Yes. He was operated on successfully

and is expected to recover. And as soon as he does, I intend to speak to him.'

'Join the queue,' Dick said.

'And meanwhile,' Maudie said, her eyes sparkling, 'Mrs. Croome will be taking her daughter and grandchild home with her as soon as they've been given the green light to leave hospital, which should be in time for Christmas.'

'Thank goodness Lily Rose is all right,' Mrs Beasley said. 'I suppose that in one way we should be grateful that my plantation was robbed, or the pair of you wouldn't have gone over there today. I shudder to think of that poor child all alone there, locked inside the hut and unable to summon help. In a way, it's a miracle, don't you think, Nurse? A Christmas miracle.'

★ ★ ★

'Rover never did get his walkies, poor beast,' Dick said out of the corner of his mouth as they were driving home with Charlie and his canine friend.

Rover immediately jumped up on the

back seat and began to bark hysterically, with his tail wagging so fast that Maudie thought he might be in danger of dislocating it. Charlie immediately raised his voice to add to the chorus.

'I told you not to say that word in front of the dog!' she said crossly. 'That's the second time today he's been promised an outing that hasn't materialized. How will we ever get him properly trained if he can't rely on anything we say? And look at the back window. It's all smeared where he's been panting on it.'

'All right, all right! As soon as I let you two off, I'll take him for a run. Will that suit your ladyship?'

'Only if you come in and have a look round the house first.'

'Of course I will, love, but I don't think you need to worry. I shan't be gone long, and in any case, Herod has gone to Banbury. He's not likely to come back now. Which reminds me, I'll have to phone the boss and let him know the latest.'

* * *

When lunch was over, Maudie lazed in her armchair beside the fire, half-listening to Dick as he spoke to DI Goodman on the phone.

'No, sir, I wasn't meddling in the case. The wife and I just popped over to set Mrs Beasley's mind at rest. A neighbourly gesture. Yes. Well, we happened to come across the young Croome girl in advanced labour, and my wife being a qualified midwife . . . no, I suggested that, but labour was too far advanced . . . Maudie wanted to accompany both mother and child to hospital, just to satisfy herself that all was well. Then we met Mrs Croome, and quite naturally Maudie wanted to speak to her about the case . . . no, no, sir! Not the police investigation. I meant the delivery of the grandchild, and so on. Yes, I'm sure you will. Right, sir! Will do!'

'What was all that about?' Maudie asked sleepily.

'Nothing much. The chief gave me a bit of a rocket about getting involved again when he'd told me to keep my nose out of it, but I think I managed to put him off the scent.'

'That's good, because there is no way I'm staying away from the Croomes! I still have work to do there, and if I happen to learn something of interest to the police, then that will be all to the good!'

'Just don't do anything to cause me to get kicked off the force, old girl.'

'As if I would! Your boss can't stop me thinking, though, can he? And what I want to know is — why Banbury?'

'Why not Banbury?'

'Because it's not far from Oxford, and that's where Ivan Croome's sister lives. What's the connection?'

'Does there have to be one?' Dick smiled indulgently at Maudie. Obviously her imagination was running riot. It would be funny if she managed to solve the case at a distance, so to speak. He hadn't realized until now just how much he resented DI Goodman's suggestion that he should be able to control Maudie! Of course, she shouldn't interfere in police work, but she was an intelligent woman with a mind of her own. Why shouldn't she put that intelligence to work if it helped solve the case?

Dick was well aware that his colleagues often did not pay much attention to what members of the public had to say. Of course, during an investigation they expected to have their questions answered honestly by anyone who was in a position to know something of value, that went without saying. But when such people came out with opinions of their own, their ideas were often ignored. You couldn't blame the men on the force when that happened. They were so used to having nutters coming forward with yarns that didn't hold water.

It was for that reason that the boss hadn't put out an appeal for anyone who knew Bracken's whereabouts. Within twenty-four hours, the man would have been spotted at a hundred different places, from Land's End to John o' Groats.

As it was, the station had received numerous letters and several phone calls from local people; including a clairvoyant, who claimed to know why Father Christmas was being targeted. The one

Dick liked best had come from a woman who said that the attacker was probably red-green colourblind, and had thought he was getting rid of a leprechaun. If only English pubs could be made to stop selling Irish whiskey, the problem would go away. Chuckling to himself yet again, Dick wondered about the nationality — and, indeed, the sanity — of the letter writer.

'What are you laughing about?' Maudie wanted to know.

'Oh, nothing. I'm just having a daft half-hour. Isn't it time we went up to bed? This has been such a busy day and I'm exhausted.'

26

Maudie presented herself at the hospital during visiting hours the next afternoon.

'I hope you won't be too long,' Dick told her, 'and mind you don't get involved in anything.'

'I don't know what you mean, Dick! And if you're worried about sitting in a cold car with Charlie, drive around a bit. I haven't come all this way just to look in on Ivan Croome and tell him to get well soon!'

Dick sighed. 'Perhaps I'll go and have a cup of tea somewhere. Charlie can sit on my lap and gnaw on a rusk.'

Maudie shot him a sly grin. 'Why don't you pop into the station? I'm sure your mates will be glad to see you!'

'Oh, brilliant! And what do I say when the boss wants to know where my wife is? I can just hear him now!'

* * *

The male surgical ward held no terrors for Maudie, who had put in her time in such surroundings at her training hospital, albeit on a much larger scale. Two rows of neatly made beds, separated by a long, low cupboard in the middle of the room, were only partly occupied. As she knew, it was the policy of hospitals everywhere to send patients home in time for Christmas, and not to admit new ones other than emergencies until after the New Year.

However, those left behind would not be forgotten. All but the very ill could look forward to a lessening of ward discipline, with carol singing around the piano, visits from local choirs or drama groups, and perhaps even a jolly Father Christmas carving the turkey for their dinner. She spied a sprig of mistletoe hanging over Sister's desk, marvelling at the daring of whoever had put it there, and wondered that the hatchet-faced woman in the navy-blue uniform had allowed it to remain there!

Ivan Croome was lying in his bed with the covers pulled up to his chin. He blinked at her approach and waved a gnarled hand as if to ward her off. 'So it's you again!' he growled. 'I got nothing to say to you, woman, so you may as well clear off right now!'

'Is that any way to greet a visitor, Mr Croome? Courtesy costs nothing, although I doubt you know what that means. The least you can do is listen to what I have to say.'

'I'm a sick man. I could be dying, for all you know. Can't you let me spend my last hours in peace?'

'Nonsense. You had a hernia repaired, and you're on the mend now. And if you suffered pain with it, it's your own silly fault. You should have gone to see the doctor as soon as you had the accident. Now, then. I want to talk to you about little Grace.'

'I don't know no Grace.'

'I had the privilege of bringing your brand new granddaughter into the world yesterday, Mr Croome. Don't you want to know how your daughter is doing?'

'I have no daughter, missus.'

'You can stop talking like that, for a

start. She's a very young girl who has made one silly mistake. Doesn't your church believe in Christian forgiveness? Right, then, don't answer me if that's the way you feel. Let's talk about something else, shall we?'

'I ain't got nothing to say.'

'Never mind. You'll have plenty of time to think about it when you're in prison.'

'Prison!'

'Well, yes. The judge is likely to send you down for a long stretch when it all comes out about what you've done. And I'm not just talking about the theft of a few pine trees, although I must say I'm surprised at you there, Mr Croome. You pretend to be such an upstanding citizen, yet you think nothing of robbing a good and generous employer.'

'I had nothing to do with them trees. That was all down to Sam Bracken.'

'But you knew what he was up to and did nothing to stop him, didn't you?'

Croome was silent, plucking at the bedclothes with restless fingers.

'What did he do, threaten to harm your wife?'

'Not her.'

'Who, then? Lily Rose?'

He nodded. 'Terrible things, he said. Things I won't repeat. I tried to knock him down, bash his teeth in, but I didn't have the strength. Threw me to the ground, he did; kicked me in the ribs while I was lying there. Then he laughed. The missus and me, we didn't know where the girl had gone; but Bracken, he told me he knew where she was staying, and that if I didn't keep quiet it would be the worse for her.'

Maudie sensed that there was more than the poaching of a few trees behind this, but she let it pass for the moment. She wanted to follow this thread to the end. 'It was you, wasn't it, Mr Croome. You are the man who's been attacking Father Christmas.' She half expected him to deny it, but instead he looked at her with watery blue eyes, his head nodding slowly.

'Well, I hope you know the trouble you're in. Attacking a retired police sergeant is a risky business. Nobody in authority is about to let that go by unpunished.'

'That was a mistake. I thought it was Alf Morton, didn't I?'

'And here's another thing! The chap lay in a coma for days in this very same hospital. If he'd died, they'd have given you an appointment with the hangman.'

'I didn't set out to kill anyone,' Croome whimpered. 'Besides, he's all right now, ain't he? Strutting around, selling them trees and pocketing the cash. He deserved a good thumping. Be sure your sin will find you out. Never was a truer word spoken.'

Maudie glanced at the clock. Visiting hour was almost over, and if she didn't finish what she'd come to do, it would soon be too late. She had learned one or two things that would be of use to Dick and he could follow them up later.

'Wait here!' she told him, which she thought afterwards was a silly thing to have said. Obviously the man was in no condition to leave his bed, even if he had entertained any thoughts of doing a bunk dressed in green-and-blue-striped pyjamas.

★ ★ ★

'Oh, hello, Nurse! Have you come to see Grace?' Lily Rose looked up from the magazine she was reading, her eyes bright.

'I'd just like to borrow her for a minute; may I?'

'I suppose so, but what . . . ?'

Maudie scooped up the little bundle from the cot at the foot of Lily's Rose's bed, and marched back down the long corridor leading back to the men's ward.

'Here,' she said, depositing the baby in her grandfather's lap, holding her hands at the ready in case he made any sudden moves. 'This is your grandchild, Mr Croome. And before you make any silly remarks about this being a child of sin, just look at her innocent little face. She's only just come into this world of ours, and it all depends on you what she'll make of it all while she's growing up. Do as I say, Mr Croome. Look at your granddaughter!'

A tear rolled slowly down his weather-beaten cheek as he stared down at the baby. Reaching out a tentative finger to touch the child, he jumped slightly when her tiny hand took it in a firm grip. A cascade of tears fell on her downy head. 'Our Lily Rose used to do that when she was this one's age,' he told Maudie, in a voice husky with emotion.

She longed to say something more, to extract a promise from him to take Lily Rose and her baby back into his home; but she was afraid to go too far and perhaps undo her good work. Instead, she picked up the baby, and suggested that he make a clean breast of the Father Christmas affair and all that lay behind it.

'I don't want to see that Goodman chap,' he muttered, as if he really had any choice in the matter. 'A right cold mortal that one is, with eyes that look straight through you. I wouldn't mind if that chap of yours came to see me, though. The wife told me how he helped save our girl. Maybe we owe him summat for that.'

'My husband, you mean? I'm afraid he's been taken off the case, Mr Croome.'

'Why's that, then? Don't tell me he's blotted his copybook in some way.'

'I'm afraid my husband isn't too happy about the way you people kidnapped our son; not to mention the threats we've been getting about the harm that may come to him in the future.'

Croome's mouth dropped open. 'Oh, I had no part of that, missus! I haven't heard nothing about no kidnapping of babies!'

The sister at the desk rang her bell vigorously and the visitors began standing up to go. 'I must get this child back to its mother,' Maudie murmured. 'I hope you'll think seriously about the things I've said, Mr Croome. It's for your own good, you know!' Cradling little Grace in her arms, she strode out of the ward without a backward glance.

27

Another frosty morning. Maudie had woken up at three a.m., needing to fumble her way to the bathroom, and she had been unable to get back to sleep. That would teach her to drink tea late at night, she told herself. By five o'clock, the idea of more tea held a certain appeal, so she got up again, wincing when her bare feet touched the cold linoleum. They really must replace the bedside rug before winter was out. The ancient rag mat that Maudie had had for years had been thrown out when Rover had been sick on it.

Having found her slippers, Maudie tiptoed downstairs, not wanting to wake Dick or the baby. Rover greeted her with a frenzy of tail-wagging and she let him out of the back door, warning him not to be long. Within minutes he was back, holding up one paw to let her know how cruel she was to send a poor dog outside on such a cold morning. She handed him a dog biscuit and he carried it back to his bed where, after crunching his prize, he sat upright, gazing at her with sad eyes. He finally accepted the fact that no more treats were forthcoming, and laid himself down with a thump and a moan.

Cupping her hands around a mug of scalding tea, Maudie wondered what the day might bring. She knew that Dick meant to telephone DI Goodman to report what she had learned from her visit to Ivan Croome; she hoped that it wouldn't bring his boss's wrath down on his head. He must stress that she had gone to the hospital to see the young mother whose baby she had delivered — and if she had acted in the best interests of the child by attempting to make peace in its family, that could be said to be part of her job, Surely Bob Goodman would see it that way? He was, after all, a father himself.

Behind her, Rover stood up suddenly, the fur on his neck bristling. He padded towards her, a low growl rumbling in his throat. She looked at him in surprise.

'What's the matter with you, boy? I don't want you waking the master. He needs his sleep.'

The dog gave another growl, louder than the first.

'Good dog, Rover. Lie down!'

The dog ignored her, springing up onto the window seat, where he wormed his way under the heavy curtain to look out over the street. Maudie's heart thumped uncomfortably. Should she awaken Dick to warn him of possible danger lurking outside? The decision was taken out of her hands when the dog began to bark. Dick appeared at the head of the stairs, yawning. He had run his fingers through his greying hair so that it stood on end, making him look like an ageing lion.

'Wassamatter?'

'Hush, mind you don't wake Charlie!' It was too late. A wail came from above. She raised her voice to make herself heard above the din. 'I don't know what's going on out there, but I could have sworn I heard a sheep.'

'Baa!'

'There it is again!'

'Probably broken through a fence somewhere and escaped. Hardly a police matter. I'm going back to bed. Do you want me to change the baby first?'

Tutting, Maudie opened the front door to look out, pulling it to behind her to avoid letting Rover escape. If the lost sheep belonged to a neighbour, they'd get no thanks if their dog chased the wayward animal, sending it on a headlong flight into the next parish!

She now saw that the bleating was coming from three ewes, herded down Llandy-fan's main thoroughfare by a well-trained collie who kept them moving in the direction he wished them to go. She recognized old Shep, Oliver Bassett's faithful dog; and then the man himself appeared around the bend in the road, stepping out at a brisk pace in mud-spattered wellies.

'Morning, Nurse! You're up early on this fine morning! No rest for the wicked, eh?'

'Same to you, Mr Bassett. What on earth are you up to?'

'Just taking these beasts to the pen at the church, ready for the Christmas pageant. Thought I'd get them settled in a couple of days early so they can get used to the place. We don't want them all agitated and complaining, drowning out the singing. Besides, the youngsters will enjoy seeing them here, I know.'

'Will they be all right on their own?'

'Of course. I brought their fodder down in the van yesterday, and the vicar said he'll keep an eye on their water trough. Easy peasy!'

'I'd better let you get on, then,' Maudie said. 'We'll see you on Christmas Eve, if not before.'

'Righty-ho!'

Shep and his charges had disappeared by this time, and Maudie reflected that the dog was probably clever enough to have delivered them to the church without his master in attendance. She closed the door, smiling to herself at the thought.

★ ★ ★

'I suppose I'd better phone the boss and get it over with,' Dick said later, pulling a wry face.

'Don't look so down in the mouth,' Maudie said, laughing. 'He ought to be pleased that I've done his work for him, and mind you tell him I said so!'

'Pigs might fly,' Dick muttered, 'and the less said by you, old girl, the better!'

'Only joking!'

Dick made his call, which was brief and to the point. Not really expecting praise, Maudie raised her eyebrows to him when he hung up the instrument. Dick shrugged.

'He didn't say much, one way or the other. Just that he'd put someone on to it right away.'

'Well, I like that!' Maudie muttered. 'I've cracked the Father Christmas mystery for him, and all he can say is that he'll put someone on to it? What about 'Well done, Mrs Bryant'?'

'Now, you know there has to be more to this than meets the eye. You told me yourself that you didn't like to dig too deeply, and I'm grateful that you didn't get too involved.'

Maudie made no reply but inside she was fuming. She longed to be in at the kill, so to speak.

* ★ ★ ★

Maudie stirred the soup she was making, wondering if the pearl barley in it was soft enough. She lifted a spoonful to her lips, blowing on it cautiously. Rats! There was the phone, and Dick wasn't here to answer it. Turning off the gas under her soup kettle, she dashed into the hall, snatching up the receiver on the eighth ring.

'Bryant residence!'

'Ah, Mrs Bryant. I'd like to speak to DS Bryant, please.' Maudie recognized the crisp tones of DI Goodman.

'I'm afraid he's not in at the moment.'

'I hope he hasn't gone far?'

'Just out walking the dog. If you'd care to ring back in about fifteen minutes?'

'No need for that, if you can get him to call me at the station.'

'Certainly. Goodbye, then.'

With her eyes sparkling, she relayed the message to Dick on his return. 'It sounds like things are moving. I wonder if they've got Herod in custody yet. The boss must be calling to bring you up to date. You will tell me what he says, won't you?'

What DI Goodman had to say wasn't fit for a lady's ears; but the gist of it, as Dick later reported to Maudie, was that Ivan Croome refused to say a word to DC Goodman, or indeed to anyone else on their team. 'He says he'll talk to DS Bryant, or not at all!'

'But I've been taken off the case,' Dick said smugly. 'You'll just have to put the pressure on the old boy.'

'Oh, yes? And how to you propose we might do that? We can hardly use thumbscrews on the old fool. We've threatened to put him in a nice cosy jail cell, but the doctor insists he's not fit to leave the hospital. There's only one thing for it, Bryant! You'll have to go and speak to him. Use kid gloves, mind. I want this case sewn up tight before Christmas.'

'Right, sir. I'll see what I can do.'

'I'll come with you,' Maudie said at once, on hearing this.

'Maudie!'

'Did he say I wasn't to go?'

'Well, no, but . . . '

'I just want to speak to him again about

Lily Rose and baby Grace. Please, Dick! Pretty please?'

'Oh, all right; but you must let me do the talking, do you understand?'

Maudie smiled sweetly. 'Of course, dear! I wouldn't dream of doing anything else!'

28

The ward sister regarded them with suspicion. 'Not another detective! You're the second one we've had here this morning, interrupting my routine! And are these your wife and child? I've never heard of anything so ridiculous! A police dog is one thing, but a baby?'

'You've had another baby here this morning?' Maudie asked with interest. 'Was it by any chance Mr Croome's granddaughter?'

'Yes, it was, as a matter of fact; although what that has to do with you, I can't imagine.'

Maudie favoured the stern woman with her best smile. 'Oh, I happen to be the midwife who delivered the baby. Mr Croome and his daughter have been estranged, you know, and I was very much hoping that they'd be reunited now. If Lily Rose brought little Grace to visit her father, that must be good news, surely?'

'I don't know about that,' Sister said, somewhat mollified by the presence of a fellow health professional, 'but at least he didn't send the pair of them away. Mind you, if the police have their way, this reunion may not last very long; for I understand from that lanky young constable who was here earlier that Mr Croome is accused of assault and battery, if nothing worse!'

Now it was Dick's turn to deliver an ingratiating smile. 'According to law, we are all innocent until proven guilty, Sister. I'm only here to try to get to the bottom of this case. If I might be allowed to get on with my interview, I can be out of here as soon as possible, and leave you in peace.'

'Very well. Nurse!' The sister waved imperiously at a junior nurse, who scuttled towards the wheeled screens indicated by her superior, and began to trundle one towards Ivan's bed. Dick settled Maudie and the baby on the single bedside chair, and fetched one for himself from a vacant bed nearby.

Once Ivan Croome began talking, the

words tumbled out unchecked. 'There's a gang of them at work,' he insisted. 'Sam Bracken, he's one of them, and that Alf Morton is in on it as well. And there's another chap, up Oxford way. I don't know much about him, except I heard the two of them talking — Sam and Alf, that is.'

'And what were they up to, exactly?' Dick asked. Enthralled, Maudie sat silently by with Charlie on her lap, saying nothing.

'The main thing is robbing the post office. The bulk of it happened where this chap worked in the sorting office at Oxford, see? Sam and Alf were laughing, saying it was money for old rope, the way people put cash in the post. It was just there for the taking, and the suckers deserved to lose it because they didn't know any better.'

'And Morton was part of this scheme,' Dick agreed. 'But surely it was just coincidence that he and this other chap — let's call him X, for want of a better name — were involved in the same sort of crime? For all we know, it could be going on the length and breadth of England, with all sorts of petty crooks helping themselves when the opportunity arose.'

'Oh, the three of them were in it together,' Ivan said. 'Sam and Alf and X, as you call him. They were all in Borstal together years ago, you see.'

'Borstal, eh?' Dick said thoughtfully. He was aware that many a future criminal alliance had been forged in the institutions for young offenders that were supposed to rehabilitate the inmates to make them fit for society.

'And they were all too old to serve in the war, so they stayed in England and got up to all sorts. Selling goods on the black market, looting bombed-out houses, you name it. And in case you're wondering how I come by this information, Sam Bracken used to boast about it all the times when we were sitting in that hut waiting for the rain to stop. Fair sickened me, it did, him going on like he was proud of himself.'

'So you decided to play God, did you? Instead of coming to the police like an honest citizen, you decided they had to be

255

punished and you tried to bump them off, one by one.'

'I never!'

'Then you made a jolly good attempt, Croome! First Morton and then Bracken. Quite clever, that, attacking them when they were both in costume as Father Christmas. You had us thinking it was some nutter targeting Father Christmases in general. And why poor old Sergeant Fry? He hasn't been robbing post offices, has he?'

Ivan moved restlessly in his bed. 'That was a mistake, see.'

'I should jolly well think it was! Judges come down hard on criminals attacking police officers, even if they do happen to be retired.'

'Sam told me Morton had been taken on at Bentham's. That's where he got the outfit. So I went there one day and lay in wait until he went to the gents', and then I struck him down.'

'But what did you hope to gain by it?'

'Why, I knew he had the loot at his digs. I meant to give the *Chronicle* an anonymous tip about that, and you lot would go there and find the stuff. And it worked, didn't it?'

'Not well enough,' Dick mused. 'The stuff was there, all right, but Morton kept insisting he'd been framed, and we weren't able to prove otherwise. So what did you have in mind when you went for Bracken?'

'I was trying to save our Edna.'

'You what?'

Maudie could contain herself no longer. 'Mr Croome's sister, in Oxford,' she said. 'You know, Dick; I told you about her. That's where Lily Rose went to when she disappeared from Brookfield.'

Dick flapped a hand at his wife and she subsided. Sister put her head around the screen and frowned. 'Are you almost finished, Detective Sergeant? Only the dinner trolley will be here at any moment, and Mr Croome will be wanting his meal.'

'Then I'm afraid that Mr Croome will have to wait!' Dick replied. With an exasperated sigh, the sister withdrew from sight.

'My sister is married to a bad 'un. Gets

up to all sorts, Harry does, and there's nothing she can do about it.'

'Why doesn't she leave him, then?' Maudie asked.

'Because marriage is for better or for worse, ain't it? Trouble is, poor Edna ain't never had the better, but she loves the miserable chap. Leastways, she says she does.'

'Go on,' Dick said. 'Are you saying that his mate's this chap we've been calling X?'

'Well, he has been working for the GPO, that much I do know; and according to Sam Bracken, he's got quite a few chaps working for him, doing this and that. Anything to rake the money in. And Sam said that if I know what was good for our Edna, I'd keep my mouth shut, because her man would take it out on her otherwise. He half-killed her once before, when all she did was tell him she knew he'd been pinching the money out of people's milk bottles that they'd left out on the doorstep to pay the milkman with.'

'And was it X who came out with the

scheme to sell Cora Beasley's trees on the market square in Midvale?'

'That was Sam Bracken.'

'Why am I not surprised?'

*   *   *

'I'll take you and Charlie home, and then I must go and make my report,' Dick told Maudie when they had left Ivan Croome toying with his plate of shepherd's pie and peas. 'Honestly, old girl, I wonder what makes some people tick! This Croome sets such store by being part of a strict religious sect, even to the point of throwing out his own daughter when she makes one foolish mistake, and yet he's been protecting this gang of petty crooks as if he's their blood brother. Can you credit it?'

Maudie didn't answer. Dick was a seasoned police officer; yet as a nurse and a midwife, she understood more about the lives and loves of ordinary people than he had yet learned to do. Of course Croome feared for his sister's well-being; that was only natural. And it had come out during the interview that he hadn't abandoned his daughter completely — as everyone, including his own wife, had been led to believe. He had sent her to his sister; partly because it might be a safe haven, and also because her presence there might save her uncle from doing violence to his wife where there was a witness. *Not a sensible view to take, under the circumstances*, Maudie thought; but then, Ivan Croome would never take the prize for clear thinking. Why else would he have gone about bashing costumed actors over the head?

'We still don't know who Herod is!' she blurted out. 'Who kidnapped our Charlie?'

'My money is on Bracken,' Dick said.

'But where is he? Croome only thinks he's gone to Banbury because that's where X lives. What if he's still lurking near Llandyfan?'

'You can stop worrying, love. Once I've reported all this to the boss, the local coppers will pay a visit to X and we'll bag the lot of them. And we don't have to keep calling him X, you know. This isn't one of those Agatha Christie novels you enjoy so much! He's a mate of Croome's brother-in-law, and his name is Peter Mills.'

Maudie was unable to put her finger on the reason why she was not entirely reassured by this. Once Dick had dropped her at home and left to return to Midvale, she made herself a strong cup of tea and sat down beside the fire to mull the situation over.

'All right, Rover,' she said aloud. 'So what if this Peter Mills is the mastermind behind all the trouble? It sounds as if he is a thoroughly nasty piece of work, all right, but why would he bother to come here all the way from Banbury?'

The dog placed an insistent paw on her knee. 'What's the matter with you, boy? Do you want to go out?' Rover whined and pawed her again.

Maudie sighed. 'I suppose you want a bikkie, do you?'

'Arf!' said Rover. Maudie broke off a piece of her festive shortbread and handed it to the dog, who wolfed it down and looked around for more.

'All that butter isn't good for you,' she

told him sternly. 'As soon as the holidays are over, you and I will have to go for more W-A-L-Ks for the sake of our waistlines. I still have baby fat to get rid of, you know, and it doesn't seem to want to budge! Now, go and lie down. I have to think.'

Right, then. If Mills didn't choose to come to Llandyfan himself, he would have delegated the job of frightening off the Bryants to one of his henchmen. Croome had staunchly denied having anything to do with Charlie's abduction; so that left Bracken and Morton, and Dick's money was on the former.

But where was he now? They had been told that he had hot-footed it to Banbury, but that wasn't necessarily true. And if the gang realized that the police were onto them, they might decide to strike again, for a police detective's baby would make a perfect hostage.

Spilling her tea in the process, Maudie leapt up and went to check that the doors were locked and bolted. Once again she brought out her trusty rolling pin in case anything untoward should happen before Dick returned.

29

The Bryants were preparing for bed late that night when the telephone rang. The fire had already been banked down and the house was cooling when Dick went to answer the summons. Hugging her dressing gown around her, Maudie hovered in the living room, straining her ears to hear what Dick was saying in response to whoever had rung. She prayed it wasn't more trouble.

'That's great news, chief!' Dick said. Maudie relaxed a little. 'All of them? Well, you'll be glad to get this lot sorted — and in time for Christmas, too. Maudie? Well, of course she'll be relieved. We both are. Goodnight, then, and thanks for ringing, sir. Merry Christmas to you, too.

'That was the boss,' Dick said, hanging up the phone.

'I gathered that. What did he have to say for himself?'

'Oxford have been onto us. They

surrounded the Mills' house at Banbury where they managed to net all three men: Mills, Bracken and Morton.'

'Well, thank goodness! What happens next, I wonder?'

'They'll spend Christmas as guests of His Majesty, and we'll begin unravelling the case in the New Year.'

'And Ivan Croome? What will happen to him?'

'He'll be charged as an accessory after the fact because of knowing what that trio were up to and turning a blind eye.'

'You can hardly call it that when he went around attacking them, Dick. What about attempted murder, for a start?'

Dick shrugged. 'Don't ask me. I wouldn't be surprised if the judge orders a psychiatric assessment of the chap before the case against him goes any further. Meanwhile, I suggest we toddle off to bed. It's like the North Pole down here.'

The North Pole, indeed, Maudie thought. Tomorrow would be Christmas Eve, and as far as all the kiddies were concerned, Father Christmas would be working his socks off up there, loading his sleigh with presents for good little girls and boys!

★ ★ ★

Maudie and Dick were up early in the morning, and were enjoying a leisurely breakfast when the doorbell rang. Dick opened the door to find the Reverend Harold Blunt on the doorstep, shivering in the cold.

'Vicar! Do come in! This is a surprise. I thought you'd be too busy to come calling today of all days.' Dick stood aside to let the visitor come in.

'I'm afraid this is not a social call, Mr Bryant.' The vicar rubbed his hands together to restore the circulation. Wondering what emergency had prompted the poor man to come out without gloves on such a cold day, Maudie stepped forward to offer a warming cup of tea.

'I won't say no,' the vicar admitted.

'Then come into the kitchen. It's a bit warmer in there.'

Harold Blunt sat down, still looking woebegone. 'The fact is, Bryant, we've had rustlers.'

'Rustlers?' Dick let out a guffaw, choking off his laughter when it dawned on him that the man wasn't joking. 'What on earth do you mean? This isn't the Wild West!'

'Nevertheless, they've been here. They've stolen Bassett's sheep from under our very noses.'

'You mean the flock he's left here as part of the school's nativity presentation?'

'Hardly a flock, being only three sheep. Still, that's three too many, wouldn't you say?'

'And when did you discover they were missing, Vicar?'

'First thing this morning, when I went out to check their water trough. The water in my drinking glass on my bedside table froze overnight, and I was afraid the animals wouldn't be able to get themselves a drink. But when I went out, I found that all was quiet, the gate wide open, and the sheep gone.'

'I see. Is it possible that the sheep could

have managed to open the gate them-selves? Or perhaps they were visited yesterday evening by local youngsters who had gone there to pet the beasts.'

'I doubt it. The men who built the pen made a point of making it escape-proof, and in any case there are ruts in the ground where some heavy vehicle has recently backed up to the gate.'

'And of course, we know that they weren't delivered in a lorry or van,' Maudie said, 'because we saw Mr Bassett and Shep delivering them on foot.'

The vicar had no sooner gone on his way, relieved to have shuffled off the responsibility onto the long arm of the law, when the doorbell pealed again. 'This is going to be one of those days, I can tell,' Dick muttered, as he went to answer it again.

This time, a plump woman wearing a shabby coat over a wraparound apron shoved her way in, pushing a reluctant child in front of her: a boy of perhaps nine or ten years old.

'Just you tell the policeman what you told me, James Matcham, or you'll get a clip round the ear like you never had before!'

Once again, Maudie surmised that this was an occasion when tea was called for to defuse the situation. She quickly fetched an extra cup for the indignant Mrs Matcham, who accepted it wordlessly; then she looked enquiringly at the child, who shook his head.

'Got any pop?'

'Got any pop, *please*,' his mother told him, before Maudie could explain that they had nothing like that in the house.

'Now then, Mrs Matcham,' Dick began. 'You have something you'd like to tell us?'

'It's about that day when your baby was snatched,' she said, pausing to drain her teacup. 'My Jimmy here saw it happen. The little varmint had bunked off school, and he was playing about in that field opposite, where he never should have been at that time of day.'

'I told you, Mum! I didn't see it happen. Not when she picked the baby up out of the pram.'

'As good as!'

'I saw her running up the road past here. That's when she must've put the kid in the manger where it was found, see?'

Maudie felt a crushing sense of disappointment. She so badly needed to know the truth about her son's abduction, for only then could she rest easy, knowing that the kidnapper was safely behind bars. She sent a miserable look in Dick's direction.

'I'm afraid you've got it wrong, son,' Dick told the boy. 'We know that our baby was stolen by a man, you see. Don't worry, you've made an honest mistake. There are plenty of ladies with babies here in Llandyfan. What you saw was someone out doing her shopping, that's all.'

'That's daft, mister. She didn't have no pram, nor a shopping basket. How would she get her stuff home like that? Besides, she was running away from the shop when I saw her.'

'Are you sure it was a woman and not a man, Jimmy?' Maudie asked. The child looked at her scornfully.

'Of course I'm sure. It was the way she

was running, see, like she couldn't bend her knees.' He turned to look at Dick. 'You know what I'm talking about, don't you, mister? You must have seen women running for the bus? Their legs go all sort of twinkling, 'specially when they have those shoes with high heels, like this one did. That's why women don't play football, see? They're made so they can't run proper.'

'You watch your lip, James Matcham, or you'll feel the weight of my hand!' his charming mother warned him. Dick raised his hand to stop the flow.

'Jimmy, I want you to listen to me very carefully. I want to make absolutely sure there's no mistake, because convicting the person responsible may depend on what you say. In fact, you may well be called upon to give evidence in court about this.'

'Cor, yes!' the boy breathed. 'Wait till they hear about this at school!'

'Well, now. Is there any other reason why you feel it may have been — only may have been, mark you — my little boy that woman was carrying?'

'Because of her!' The boy pointed a

finger at Maudie. 'I saw you, missus — and that dog there — coming along right after the other woman went by. That dog knew she was the kidnapper, else why did he get right on her trail and keep yelping the way he did? Dogs know, you know!'

'But why didn't you come and tell us this days ago?' Maudie demanded. 'It would have saved us all a lot of grief.'

'Obvious, innit?' Mrs Matcham said, curling her lip. 'The little bleeder didn't want me to find out he'd been bunking off school. It wasn't till that Miss Probert stopped me in the street that I cottoned on to what he'd been up to. 'I do hope young James is feeling better now,' says she. 'It's too bad to take sick right at Christmastime; he'll miss all the fun.' Well, when I got my hands on him, he remembered what he'd seen in a hurry; so here we are, and I hope it's been a help to you.'

'More than you'll ever know,' Dick told her.

The last they heard as mother and son walked away from the cottage was the boy's loud complaints. 'It's not fair, Mum! I solved their case for them, and they didn't even give me a glass of pop for coming clean!'

'I'll give you pop!' she roared. Her son dodged away from her, neatly avoiding her avenging hand.

30

'I'll swing for that Mrs Croome,' Maudie howled. 'After all I've done for her! Going to bat for her, trying to help find her missing daughter. Bringing her grandchild into the world after the woman was foolish enough to lock Lily Rose in an isolated hut, far too close to her time. And then how does she reward me? By stealing my baby and almost giving me a heart attack, never mind all the stress that put us through later.'

'Charlie was kidnapped before you did any of that,' Dick pointed out.

'So what? It's the principle that matters. And I suppose she wrote those threatening notes, too. Was she in the pay of this Peter Mills, or did she just want to protect her husband from what he had coming to him?'

'I don't know, love, but we're going to find out. I shall go and pay a call on her at Brookfield. Do you want to come too?'

'Just try leaving me behind!'

★ ★ ★

Mrs Croome greeted them brightly when she saw who was at her door. 'I'm ever so glad you're here,' she said, as they followed her into her shabby kitchen. 'Now I'm able to thank you in person! Ivan says our Lily Rose can move back in, and the baby too. It's what I was hoping for all along, but I never thought it would happen. It's like a miracle, and I'm so grateful!'

'You've got a funny way of showing it, then,' Maudie said, unable to keep the bitterness out of her tone. 'How dare you steal this baby of mine? Anything could have happened!'

Mrs Croome turned pale. 'Oh, no, that weren't me!'

'It wasn't? Then who . . . '

'It was our Edna, Ivan's sister.'

'Look, do you mind if we all sit down?' Dick asked. 'We've all had a bit of a shock this morning, and there are one or two things that need to be sorted out.'

When they were all seated, and the visitors had refused the offer of tea or a glass of water (good for shock, their hostess informed them), Dick started again.

'Tell me about Edna, Mrs Croome. Your sister-in-law.'

'She's not a bad person, Mr Bryant. But that man of hers is a real villain, and she's afraid to speak out of turn for fear she'll come to harm. Well, I didn't go to Edna's like I said before. They turned up here in that old van of theirs with Harry's mate, that Peter Mills. Peter, he starts off saying that their whole business is about to go down the drain because some pesky detective — only that wasn't the word he used — some pesky detective is on the verge of making a deduction that can send them all down for a long stretch. He told me he wanted me to snatch your boy. I told him where he could go with his evil notions, and that's when he told me that if I didn't do as he said, our Lily Rose would pay. He'd kill her baby, and that would serve me right, he said. Well, that nearly froze my blood in my veins, I can tell you, but I managed to refuse again. Well, you have to stand up to bullies, don't you? For all I knew, he meant to kill both babies, your boy and Lily Rose's as well!'

'Herod!' Maudie murmured.

'What?'

'And then what happened?' Dick prompted.

'Poor Edna spoke up and said she'd do it. So I managed to get her on her own, and I told her how to find the church, where she could leave the little boy in the manger and hope he'd be found in time. Off they went in the van, and they must have hung about for days until at last they saw you setting off with the pram and saw their chance. Peter put Edna off round the corner and drove off into the countryside in case someone noticed the van and took down the license number.

'Poor Edna saw the baby safely into the manger, and then just kept walking until Peter came and picked her up again. She was in a sorry state when they reached here, I can tell you. Blisters on her heel, and a torn skirt where that dog of yours took after her and tore a strip off it. Oh yes, he caught up with her once or twice and terrified the wits out of her. Great slavering beast, she told me, just like the Hound of the Whatsits.'

'Baskervilles,' Maudie supplied, being particularly fond of Conan Doyle's Sherlock Holmes stories. 'And he's just an ordinary little terrier-mix with the heart of a lion.'

'Whatever you say. But what will happen to her now? Poor Edna, she's had a long row to hoe, married to that brute. She won't go to prison, will she?'

'That will be for the courts to decide,' Dick told her.

'Oh, the shame and disgrace of it all!' Mrs Croome looked at Maudie. 'You will speak up for her, won't you? I know she did wrong, but she did save your little one in the end.'

'We shall have to see.' Maudie wasn't yet ready to commit herself. 'I suppose you wouldn't know anything about stolen sheep, would you?'

'Sheep? I don't know what you're

talking about, but I do know that Alf Morton has a chum called Freddie Malladine. He's a butcher down the High Street. I'd go and have a word with him, if I were you. He's got a smallholding on the road down past Cora Beasley's place. It might be worth having a look around there.'

'And we'd best do that now,' Dick told Maudie when they were in the car, pulling away from the Croomes' cottage. 'I'd like to see those sheep returned to Oliver Bassett, before they turn into mutton chops!'

Singing carols together, they went off to try to right yet another wrong.

31

Christmas Eve found the three Bryants preparing to take part in the age-old ritual of celebrating the Saviour's birth. Maudie dressed their son for the event and presented him to Dick for his inspection.

'Just look at you, all togged out!' He gently poked his son in the tummy and the baby wriggled and smiled. Young Charlie wore a brand-new red knitted suit, and all he needed was a false beard to appear as a miniature Father Christmas. Dick said as much, but Maudie only smiled. The fears that had beset them in recent weeks were gone now, and they could afford to joke about their troubles.

'We'd better get going,' Dick said, 'or we won't get a seat. I remember what it was like last year. I had to stand at the back with some of the other men. Not my idea of a comfortable evening.'

'That was when they held the concert

in the school. The parish hall is much bigger.'

'Maybe so, but don't forget we're all going straight from there into the church, which is always bursting at the seams for the carol service.'

'I want to sit at the back anyway,' Maudie said. 'Just in case Charlie gets fretful and I have to take him out. He's got his rubber pants on inside his suit because I don't want the good wool getting soaked, but they won't keep his skin dry and he may set up a howl. Roll on, potty-training!'

The school's Christmas pageant was much the same as those Maudie had attended in other years, but its charm remained undiminished. The parents were enthralled by it all, of course, although the mother of one of the older boys sat biting her nails until the child had successfully worked his way through a recitation of the Bible verses recounting how the Angel of the Lord appeared to the shepherds.

Everyone giggled when an eager child — clad in the requisite dressing gown, with a tea-towel on his head — waved frantically from his place on the floor, where he was supposed to be guarding his sheep. 'Look, Mummy! This is my lamb!' he called, holding a rather battered teddy above his head.

And when the smallest member of the infants' class staggered onto the stage holding a wand, complete with glittering star, there were cries of 'Aww! The pretty dear!' And if the wand was better suited to a fairy tale than to point to the birth of the babe at Bethlehem, what did that matter? Everyone was aware of its significance, and that was all that mattered.

Looking around him, Dick surmised that the whole village must have turned out for the occasion, as well as most of the inhabitants of the surrounding countryside. It was a good job that the rogue Father Christmases were behind bars, because this was the perfect opportunity for burglars to get to work around the district . . .

'Stop thinking about work, and just enjoy yourself!' he muttered, earning a puzzled glance from his wife.

Miss Probert's true soprano echoed round the room. *'O little town of Bethlehem, How still we see thee lie . . . '* Maudie looked at Joan Blunt who sat across the aisle, her expression rapt. Once again, the vicar's wife had managed to iron out a problem that had threatened to throw the parish into disarray, with everyone taking sides according to their inclinations. Miss Probert was singing here, in her own milieu as a teacher at the school, while Gladys Brown would perform the solo in the church, as she had done for many a year.

As it turned out, this would be her swansong, for she was soon to leave the village to go to live with her sister in Exeter. She would be presented with a gift before she left, along with a scroll of appreciation for her years of service, Honour would be satisfied all round.

Charlie wriggled in Maudie's lap, bringing her attention back to the present. Five years from now, this baby would be up on that stage with the others, acting the part of a shepherd, or even the innkeeper! Some day he might even aspire to being one of the three kings, or be chosen to read part of the Nativity story while she sat in the front row, desperately willing him not to stumble, or dry up from stage fright!

The presentation over, the headmistress rose to ask people to remain seated while the children filed out. Then they could follow the youngsters into the church, where the carol service would take place.

Maudie watched the children's faces as they passed her chair, singing 'Once in Royal David's City'. Even the naughtiest of the little rascals looked like an angel tonight, she thought. The season had wrought its magic once again.

Then they reached the manger scene where the sheep, safely restored to their owner, stood inside the railings; accompanied by a donkey, placidly watching as the procession slowly passed by. Glancing at the manger itself, Maudie breathed a little prayer of thanks for the safety of her baby. The criminal they had called Herod had not triumphed, just as the real King

Herod had failed to kill the child Jesus.

Inside the candlelit church, the organ swelled. This was a festival of carols and lessons. Taking their places, the congregation sang lustily, sitting from time to time to hear readings performed by the vicar and churchwardens. Some of these had already been performed by the children, yet the people were none the worse for hearing them again. In any case, most people there knew the words by heart, and those verses could never lose their appeal.

★ ★ ★

'Did you enjoy the concert, Nurse?'

Maudie stiffened at the sound of Mrs Hatch's voice.

'Goodwill to all men!' Dick hissed in her ear.

With a supreme effort, Maudie managed to bare her teeth. 'Lovely, yes.' Fortunately, the exodus from the church was gaining momentum, and she allowed herself to be swept down the path away from the postmistress.

'Well done, old thing!' Dick muttered.

'Oh, I'm not a candidate for sainthood yet,' she told him. 'But we *have* just come out of church, and I mean to keep hold of the holy feeling for a bit longer. Just wait till the New Year, though! Then I'm going to let her have it!'

'Don't be so hard on her, love. Think what it must be like, standing behind that counter year after year. What else does she have to look forward to, besides taking an interest in the doings of her customers?'

'Spreading gossip and false rumours, that's what. Years ago, they'd have dumped her in the duck pond for being a scold.'

'Isn't that a bit harsh? The poor soul is probably lonely.'

'Huh!' said Maudie.

★ ★ ★

Their cottage was warm and snug when they returned home. Rover, asleep in front of the banked-down fire, opened one eye, decided that all was well, and went back to sleep.

'I'll put the kettle on while you see to Charlie,' Dick said. 'Are we going to open our presents tonight, or wait until morning?' There were a number of mysterious packages beneath their little tree; and, child-like, Dick was keen to tear them open. A tiny parcel, heavy for its size, had his name on it, and he couldn't imagine what it might hold.

'Oh, in the morning, I think, don't you? I do want Charlie to be there when we do it, not that he's likely to take much of an interest at his age.'

'Right-ho.' Dick took the poker to the fire, which sprang into life, its flames casting shadows on the wall. Actually, he couldn't wait to see what Maudie made of the gifts he had bought her. Unable to reach a decision, he had consulted Joan Blunt; and, as usual, she had come up with the right answers. At least, he hoped she had!

'If you can't decide on one main gift, in case you get it wrong, why not get her several smaller things?' Mrs Blunt had suggested.

'Such as?'

'Well, now, we know she loves mystery novels. That would be a good start.'

'But how will I know which one to buy? She's always bringing home books from the library. I've no idea what she's already read.'

'Book tokens,' Mrs Blunt said. 'Buy a token in the amount you want to spend, and she can choose for herself.'

'All right, I will, but I can't help thinking it won't give her much to open on the day.'

For once the vicar's wife allowed her exasperation to show. 'You are really making heavy weather of this, you know! As I suggested, buy several things; and if you can't manage that, hide the book token in a big box filled with tissue paper. Where there's a will, there's a way!'

Dick took the hint and plumped for several items. A box of Rowntree's Black Magic chocolates; with any luck, she might let him have the marzipans and the coffee creams. A fascinating album that allowed a mother to keep a record of her baby's first five years. Surprisingly, they hadn't been given one when Charlie was born, and he knew she would love it. A cherry-red lipstick called Instant Desire. A waste of money really, when he knew he would only kiss it off the lips he loved, but so what? It was Christmas, wasn't it?

32

Maudie walked down the silent street, clutching her tweed coat around her. The night air was clear and the sky filled with what looked to her like a million stars. On such a night as this, the Magi, filled with longing, had followed some bright sign in the sky to take them to the newborn baby Jesus; *for we have seen his star in the east, and are come to worship him.*

The Bible said that *the star, which they saw in the east, went before them, till it came and stood over where the young child was.* Was it such a star as those she could see twinkling far above her — or perhaps a fiery comet, such as Halley's Comet that had appeared from time to time over the centuries? Maudie didn't know. Did anyone? Not that it mattered. The three wise men had undertaken their journey in good faith, and arrived at last in Bethlehem to bow down before the king of kings. *And when they had opened their treasures, they presented unto him gifts; gold, and frankincense, and myrrh.*

'And that is why we give each other presents at Christmas,' she recalled a long-ago Sunday-school teacher telling her pupils.

A few yards ahead of her, a gate opened and a couple came out, walking briskly in the same direction as herself. A car purred down the street, passing slowly to avoid splashing the walkers with the rainwater that had filled the gutters earlier in the day. It seemed as if everyone was bound for St John's church for the midnight service.

Despite having attended the carol service during the evening, Maudie felt she needed the spirituality and calm of the late-night ritual as well. The children's pageant had been delightful enough, yet it had secular overtones which did not quite meet her need to worship in her own way. She felt an overwhelming need to give thanks for all the gifts she had received in recent weeks; gifts that meant more to her than all the gold and jewels in the world. She wanted to sit quietly in the ancient church and think about that.

Dick had understood. 'I'll stay home with Charlie,' he said. 'We could take him with us, of course, but he's really too young to be out and about in the middle of the night, never mind the cold. I'll wait up for you, love, and I'll make you a hot toddy when you get in.'

Seeing her putting on her coat and hat, Rover had jumped up in excitement, only to lie down again when Dick summoned him back to his place on the hearthrug. The animal's disappointed moan made them both laugh. *What?* he seemed to be saying. *Walkies at this time of night, and you're not taking me? What a way to treat a poor dog!*

'Baa!' The gentle cries of sheep came to Maudie's ears as she rounded the corner past the parish hall. Yes, the three missing ewes had been returned to their pen in time for the children's pageant and the carol service, and she and Dick had been largely responsible for that. After talking to Mrs Croome, they had driven out to Cora Beasley's tree plantation — where, sure enough, they had found the beasts shut inside the very hut where Maudie had delivered baby Grace just days earlier.

Dick had then driven to police headquarters at Midvale — 'on three wheels', as Maudie described it to Joan Blunt later — and arrangements were made to apprehend the rustlers before they had a chance to slaughter the sheep. Whether the local butcher was in fact the guilty party remained to be seen. Oliver Bassett had collected the animals in his old van and returned them to the church.

St John's was already half-full when Maudie arrived. Having been handed a hymnbook and shown to a vacant pew by a sidesman, she knelt down to murmur a prayer before sitting up to look around her. The Norman church had been fitted with electricity years ago, but tonight the congregation would worship by candle-light, which added to the awe and mystery of the occasion. As she had done many times before, Maudie thought of all the men and women, ordinary people like herself, who had sat here throughout the centuries. All had come here in the joyful belief that the babe of Bethlehem was the Son of God, sent down to earth to be their saviour.

The congregation stood. Now the procession was coming down the aisle, led by a young crucifer in a white surplice. Maudie recognized him as the boy who had given one of the Bible readings in the school's Nativity pageant. Then the choir, all fully robed; including a beaming Gladys Brown, who, on this most magical night of the year, would perform her final solo in the church she had served so well for forty years. The Reverend Harold Blunt was in his element, ready to lead his flock in worship as had dozens of other clergymen before him.

In his address to the gathering that night, the vicar spoke of the great miracle being commemorated here yet again as they celebrated the birth of the Christ-child. Great happiness welled up in Maudie as she gave thanks for the other, smaller miracles that had accompanied this season. She and Dick had gone through a difficult patch in their marriage, but they were all right again now. Charlie was snug in his cot at home, when the outcome of his abduction could have been so very different.

Long ago, the evil King Herod had tried to trick the wise men into telling him where the Baby Jesus was, *that I may come and worship him also*. But the Lord had stepped in to foil his plan, for *being warned of God in a dream that they should not return to Herod, they departed into their own country another way*. And even though Rover was the hero of the hour when Charlie was kidnapped, Maudie was in no doubt that some guardian angel had inspired Edna to disobey her husband's partner in crime: that nasty piece of work known to the Bryants, for a time, as a modern-day Herod.

And, as Maudie had long ago decided, divine providence was often at work in the world, using ordinary men and women to bring about small miracles. She herself had been brought to the foresters' hut in Lily Rose's hour of need so that mother and baby had come safely through their ordeal. And now the girl's stern father had been prevailed upon to let his daughter and grandchild take up residence under his roof, which was a small miracle in itself! Whether Ivan Croome would be present to share that home was a matter for the courts to decide, but that was another story.

Up in the belfry the great bells began their joyous clanging, sending their message out over the surrounding countryside. *Christ is born! Christ is born!* Not so long ago, the ringing of church bells had been banned, for during the war it had been decreed that they should only be used to warn people that the promised invasion had started, if other communications had been cut off. Now they were at peace again, but Maude would never forget that grim morning when the vicar had announced that Britain was at war with Germany. She had looked around the ancient building with growing dismay. Centuries ago, it had somehow escaped the attention of Oliver Cromwell and his minions, but she lived in a different time.

Would St John's be destroyed by bombing? But it had survived, when many others had not.

Having been seated near the front of the church, Maudie was among the last to leave. She could hear the cries of departing folk outside as they called greetings to one another. *Happy Christmas! Happy Christmas!*

Now it was her turn to leave for home. Pausing on the steps for a moment, she looked up into the sky as the first snowflakes began to fall. It looked as if it would be a white Christmas after all. With a thankful heart, Maudie Bryant turned her face towards home, where the people she loved awaited her.

We do hope that you have enjoyed reading this large print book.

Did you know that all of our titles are available for purchase?

We publish a wide range of high quality large print books including:
Romances, Mysteries, Classics
General Fiction
Non Fiction and Westerns

Special interest titles available in large print are:
The Little Oxford Dictionary
Music Book, Song Book
Hymn Book, Service Book

Also available from us courtesy of Oxford University Press:
Young Readers' Dictionary
(large print edition)
Young Readers' Thesaurus
(large print edition)

For further information or a free brochure, please contact us at:
Ulverscroft Large Print Books Ltd.,
The Green, Bradgate Road, Anstey,
Leicester, LE7 7FU, England.
Tel: (00 44) **0116 236 4325**
Fax: (00 44) **0116 234 0205**